The Legend of
Daisy Flowerdew

The Legend of Daisy Flowerdew

PATRICIA PENDERGRAFT

PHILOMEL BOOKS
New York

Copyright © 1990 by Patricia Pendergraft.
First published in the United States of America
in 1990 by Philomel Books, a division of
The Putnam & Grosset Group, 200 Madison Avenue,
New York, NY 10016. All rights reserved.
Published simultaneously in Canada.
Book design by Gunta Alexander.
Printed in the United States of America.

Library of Congress Cataloging-in-Publication Data
Pendergraft, Patricia.
The legend of Daisy Flowerdew / by Patricia Pendergraft.
p.   cm.   Summary: Misunderstood and unwanted by her pretty
mother and stepfather, thirteen–year–old Daisy Flowerdew
finds solace in two magical paper dolls.
ISBN 0-399-22176-X
[1. Family problems—Fiction.   2. Dolls—Fiction.
3. Country life—Fiction.]   I. Title.
PZ7.P3735Le   1990   [Fic]—dc20   89-37004   CIP   AC
First Impression.

*For Richard, Theresa, Steve and Lisa,
Heidi, Tammy and Jeff and, of course,
the babies, Drew and Ty.*

The Legend of Daisy Flowerdew

Chapter
One

The awkward sign propped up in the window of Heath's Dry Goods Store read:

MARRY DAISY FLOWERDEW AND
MAKE YOURSELF TEN DOLLARS

Beneath these words Delbert Heath had scrawled in big round uncertain letters: "Inquire Within." A black hand with a long finger pointed to the door of the store.

Not many folks had "inquired within" except out of curiosity and, of the few eligible young men in Vineyard Flats who had, not one had taken up the offer. Only Elmer Goots from out south of town had shown the least bit of interest in the proposition. And that was more because of the ten dollars old man Heath was offering than the prospect of marrying thirteen-year-old Daisy Flowerdew. The truth was, Elmer wasn't ready to marry any girl. But he was ready to latch onto a quick ten dollars if he could.

Delbert Heath was Daisy's stepfather, a fact he hadn't been aware of when he married her mother, Jessee. If Jessee hadn't kept Daisy hidden away the way she had, Delbert might not have married Jessee at all. A woman like Jessee, though, was pretty hard for a man like Delbert Heath to resist. She had an angel's face, hair as white as bleached sheets on a sunny day, and a little girl's way of talking that made Delbert's heart do flip-flops in his thin chest. He had never known of any woman to talk the way Jessee did. Some folks said old man Heath went "hog wild" over Jessee. But they had to admit, she was the most fascinating female to ever walk down the dusty streets of Vineyard Flats.

Jessee had kept Daisy over in Punkin Center with her mother for close to ten years. Punkin Center was some thirty-odd miles away from Vineyard Flats and a safe distance as far as Jessee was concerned. But, when her mother passed on and no other relatives were willing to take up bearing the cross of Daisy, Jessee was compelled to take the girl and admit to her husband, Delbert, that she existed.

Few folks in Vineyard Flats remembered Daisy. Those who did recalled a chubby little tyke with dark, almost black hair, a round homely face with distinct, sharp-looking features, and dark eyes that stared long and hard at everything she looked at. At three years of age, she did not even mumble or attempt a word. "The young'un ain't right," Jessee admitted to herself in horror. "She ain't right and I ain't keeping her!"

"Ain't no one wants a young'un like Daisy!" Jessee's brother Flint, from over in Punkin Center, told her.

"That young'un was created in sin!" Flint's wife, Lou, said scornfully while eyeing the child with contempt.

"Hush your mouth, Lou!" Granny Henry had exploded as she ripped the forlorn-looking child up from the floor and held her tightly in her thin arms. "*I'll* take this baby!" she said, tossing her head back with determination and an accusing look all around the room.

Granny Henry took Daisy that very day back to Punkin Center to her home and cared for her until the day she died. It was Granny Henry who gave Daisy her last name after Jessee insisted she didn't want the child to carry her name. Daisy loved the flowers that grew in Granny Henry's yard and after many failed attempts, Granny was at last able to teach her to say the word "flower." And because Daisy was so fascinated with the bright balls of morning dew that sat precariously on the tips of the petals Granny Henry told her, "That's what I'm going to call you, child. Little Daisy Flowerdew. That's your name from now on."

Jessee married Delbert and moved clear away from Hoosier City. It was only when Granny Henry died that the strapping girl with the penetrating eyes and the young boyish face returned to her mother and was plunked down to live in the back porch of the house Delbert and Jessee lived in on Dogtown Road, right there in Vineyard Flats. Jessee and Delbert had been married exactly one year.

"You sure that young'un of yourn is a girl?" Delbert had asked Jessee the moment he laid eyes on Daisy for the first time. Daisy was setting at the breakfast table in the kitchen her first morning in her new home. She looked down quickly when Delbert spoke and stared at the little dark spots of spilled coffee on the linoleum floor.

"Why, of course, honey bear," Jessee cooed, looking up at her husband with her bright blue eyes wide and her eyelashes fluttering.

Delbert shook his head and stared gravely at Daisy, who was wearing the long bib overalls, dark flannel shirt, and Uncle Flint's cast-off brogans that she had always worn at Granny Henry's. She knew her stepfather was studying her closely. She could feel his eyes moving over her critically as she concentrated on the shape of the coffee spills. They were all in spattery little circles and she counted four.

"She sure looks like a boy to me," Delbert said, rubbing his chin.

"Well, honey bear, wouldn't I know?" Jessee asked, flashing her eyes uncomfortably over Daisy, then back at Delbert with a forced smile on her pretty lips. Her heart fluttered with fear. The same fear that had haunted her ever since she first realized Daisy was so different. That somehow, someway, Daisy would ruin everything in life for her. That Daisy could, just by her peculiar presence, ruin her marriage and her good secure life with her husband, and Jessee would be transported back into what she was before she met Delbert . . . a poor, down-on-her-luck waitress living from hand to mouth and with no one to love her.

"I reckon you would at that," Delbert admitted with a raw chuckle.

"Well, sure I would, honey bear," Jessee cooed with relief while flickering her eyelashes over her husband's face.

"The thing is, how come her to look like that?" Delbert persisted the next time he saw Daisy, which was the second morning she appeared at the breakfast table. He leaned against the counter in the kitchen, his coffee cup in hand, studying Daisy exactly as he had the day before.

Daisy's eyes zoomed to a corner of the kitchen where Jessee had plunked a large cactus plant into an old wash tub filled with dirt, and stayed there.

"Well . . . well, honey bear, Daisy just . . . she just *happened!*" Jessee answered helplessly.

Daisy had already been cautioned by Jessee to stay out of Delbert's way as much as possible. She was allowed to appear at the breakfast table in the mornings, but told to stay in her porch bedroom when Delbert came home from work at the end of the day.

"It ain't that I'm trying to *hide* you, Daisy," Jessee had tried to explain with her words fumbling over each other. "After all, we *are* a family. But, you see, you ain't exactly *Delbert's* family. What I'm trying to say is, you ain't his own blood ken like you are mine. He never had no young'uns and he don't know exactly what to make of having a young'un as big as you are around the house. He never married me expecting you'd come along and move in on us, Daisy. He expected we'd be alone. Just him and me living here all by ourselves. Well, what I'm *trying* to tell you is, it might be best if you'd just sort of not come around Delbert too much. Just kind of stay in your room when he's at home." Jessee stopped, waiting for some response from Daisy, but when none came, she went on, her voice rising with emotion. "This is the first and only chance I ever had at having a real marriage and a home of my own, Daisy, and I ain't aiming to let no one, not even you, take it away from me! You just got to stay out of the way!" Jessee reached out and grabbed both of Daisy's arms and held them tightly.

Jessee was sure that she had said it all wrong and she wasn't even certain that Daisy understood. All the girl had done, the whole time Jessee had been talking, was to stare deeply and blankly into her eyes. And even when she grabbed her arms, all Daisy had done was continue to stare.

It made Jessee feel uncertain and uncomfortable, as though there were a huge space between them that neither one could penetrate. As the days passed, Daisy's appearance in the house became less and less. She spent most of her time in her room staring up at the raw, splintery wood of the ceiling or walking in the woods down by Toby's Creek, where the bird songs mingled with the breezes sighing through the pine trees and the rustle of small animals making paths through the fallen leaves.

It was at Toby's Creek that Daisy spoke her first words in Vineyard Flats. And, when she did, it was to the sparrows, the jays, and the robins that perched in the tree branches above her head.

"I wish I wasn't here," she told them, her head thrown back and her black hair hanging to her waist in long uncombed tangles. "I wish I was still with Granny Henry." But speaking Granny Henry's name only made the pain she felt inside more immense.

"Granny Henry is dead. Granny . . . is . . . dead. . . ," she would often say slowly to herself, as if trying to make it all real to her. But, somehow, it never was.

Chapter
Two

After Daisy had been in Vineyard Flats for a while, some of the ladies of the town decided to pay a visit on Jessee to meet her daughter. It would be a good idea, they thought, to invite both of them to church, seeing as how Jessee herself hardly ever went. Also, they were getting curious about Daisy, since Jessee never appeared in town with her and when they met her on the street and inquired about the girl, Jessee always mumbled vaguely, looked embarrassed, and glanced away.

It was a Saturday afternoon when Cooney Rawls, Nudie Johnson, and Beadie Brown walked up on the front porch of the house with covered dishes in their hands and rapped on the door. Jessee, primping in a hand mirror while singing along with T. Texas Tyler on the radio, reluctantly snapped off the radio, got up, and went to the door. When she saw the three ladies standing there, she shoved the hand mirror behind her back and said an embarrassed "Oh!"

"How do, Jessee," Cooney Rawls said brightly and her smile brought all the wrinkles on her face together in a mass of little highways, hills, and dales.

"We come to meet your girl, Jessee," Nudie Johnson said. Nudie had a noticeable bald spot in the very front of her hair. She tried to cover it by sweeping a mound of hair from the side over it, but it always showed through and was a conversation piece among the children of the town.

"Oh!" Jessee said again, blinking her eyes in embarrassment as Beadie Brown said, "And we've brought some cobbler and pies." Beadie was very fat and very short with little eyes just like her name.

"Oh!" Jessee muttered for a third time, feeling the hand mirror tremble in her hands behind her back.

"Ain't you going to invite us in, Jessee?" Cooney asked, trying to peer around Jessee and see into the front room.

"Oh . . . well . . . ummm . . . well, why sure," Jessee managed to say as she reached for the latch on the screen door while still hanging onto the mirror behind her with her other hand.

The ladies trooped inside and headed straight for the kitchen, where they placed the dishes of cobbler and pies on the table. Jessee quickly laid the mirror on the table beside the radio and hurried into the kitchen behind the ladies. They were already setting around the table when she entered the room.

"That coffee over yonder on the stove sure does look inviting," Cooney said and Nudie and Beadie agreed with smiles and nods of their heads.

Jessee nervously set about getting cups, saucers, and forks and placed them in front of the ladies. All the while her mind was on Daisy.

"Call that girl of yourn in here, Jessee," Beadie said suddenly. "We want to meet her."

"And invite her over to the church. They is lots of nice young boys that would like to get acquainted with a new girl," Nudie said and all the ladies laughed.

"Well. . . ," Jessee said as she poured the coffee into the cups. Her hands shook and the coffee sloshed into the saucers.

"We won't touch a bite ner take a sip until you come back with her," Beadie said and the ladies laughed again.

Jessee left the kitchen feeling sick with shame that she would have to bring Daisy out and introduce her to the women. How would she do it and what was she going to say? Oh, why did the meddling old fools have to come? she wondered angrily. Her heart ached for Daisy, but, oh, why did she have to be born? *Why?* It was the same question she had been asking forever, it seemed. She opened the door to the back porch and saw Daisy lying on her bed looking up at the ceiling.

"Daisy?" she asked softly so the ladies wouldn't hear.

Daisy continued to stare at the ceiling. Jessee approached the bed and looked down at her. "Daisy, they is some ladies from town who want to meet you. Come into the kitchen with me. You won't have to stay long. They want to see . . ." Jessee stopped on the word "see." Yes, she thought bitterly, they only wanted to *see* Daisy! And what would they say and think once they saw her?

Daisy's eyes moved from the ceiling to Jessee's face filled with fear. "Come on now, Daisy," Jessee said. "The sooner you meet them, the sooner it will be over and you can come back here and lay down."

Daisy refused to budge from the bed. "Come *on*!" Jessee pleaded, trying to keep her voice low so the ladies in the kitchen would not hear. But Daisy wouldn't move. "Damn you!" Jessee exploded as she reached for the girl and yanked, pulled, and drug her up from the bed. Daisy drew back, but Jessee would not let go of her. "Now, you just get yourself in there and greet them old crows and you can come back here and lay in bed all day long, for all I care!" Jessee gasped and sputtered as she shoved Daisy through the door into the kitchen.

"Here she is," she said, trying to sound composed, but her face was a blotch of red, and her hair had flown in all directions from her struggle with Daisy.

The three women turned their heads to look at Daisy. The smiles they had prepared on their faces quickly faded and their eyes turned hard as they surveyed Daisy up and down, up and down, like a sharp edge of glass slicing over her. Up and down, up and down until, finally, their eyes stopped and stared deeply into her face. Daisy stood like a statue, her arms hanging at her sides, her shoulders scrunched up close to her neck, her eyes large and filled with terror. Inside her overalls her legs jiggled against the rough fabric. Inside her flannel shirt her arms moved in spasms. And her feet, inside Uncle Flint's brogans, felt cemented to the floor.

Suddenly Daisy's mind flashed with the memory of a time just like this, when Granny Henry had decided to send her to school. She was twelve then, much older than the other children, who were several years younger. She had stood in the play yard watching hungrily as the other children played among themselves, throwing balls, playing tag, running in all directions, shouting and calling out to one another. Their laughter was like a beautiful song and she had longed to join in with them, to become a part of what they were. Her great round eyes roved over each face, as though she were trying to drink in all that they were and she had never been.

As suddenly as the drop of a pin, the school yard became still and quiet. The faces of the children turned toward Daisy, glaring at her first with puzzlement, then with contempt and hatred for all her fearsome strangeness. She pleaded with her eyes for them to speak to her, to smile at her, to invite her to play with them. But no one did. They moved silently toward her, their hatred beaming out at her like the sun had fallen from the sky and was burning over every part of her. A small, scrawny boy raised his fist and shook it at her and shouted, "You get out of here!" Soon the other children joined in, yelling and screaming and calling her names. She turned and ran, with the sound of their beautiful laughter turned into taunting mockery.

That very evening, angry parents came to Granny Henry's and demanded that she keep Daisy away from their school and away from their children. "We don't want that one around our young'uns!" they said, with their evil hatred permeating every corner of Granny Henry's house. When they had gone, Granny Henry put her arms around Daisy and held her for a long, long time. Then she let her go and looked into her eyes. "Daisy, I wanted to send you to school so's you could get some book learning. So's you wouldn't be alone in your mind. But folks won't let you be. They fear you because you're different, child. As different as the hoot owl is from the blue bird. It ain't your fault. It ain't no one's fault. Only the Lord knows why he done this." Granny Henry sighed then and pulled Daisy back into her arms.

Daisy's head swam with strangeness, with the profound feeling of being "different," and of wondering why she was and not knowing. It was the same way she felt now, with the eyes of the three women rolling over her and the expression on their faces filled with puzzlement and distaste.

"This is Daisy," Jessee said, writhing with embarrassment and hating the ladies because they had come.

"Let us hear your voice, child," Nudie Johnson said at last, with the sound and look of suspicion emanating from her.

"Yes," Beadie said, leaning across the table, her eyes narrowed and her head tilted expectantly.

Suddenly Daisy sprang from the kitchen, leaped

across the house, and burst out the front door. She was down the steps and out of the yard before the ladies at the table knew what was happening. She ran and ran until she reached Toby's Creek and dropped into the mossy grass. Above her in the trees the bob-whites chattered and the jays argued loudly, a squirrel ran up and down a nearby tree trunk, and the water in the creek lapped gently against the soft dirt bank. Daisy clutched a fistful of grass in her hand and hammered it into the ground over and over again.

Chapter
Three

It didn't take long for word to spread over Vineyard Flats about that peculiar child of Jessee Heath's. Gossip moved fast and furiously, from tongue to tongue and house to house, until Delbert began to feel self-conscious and angry about the strange, silent, boyish creature that belonged to his wife.

One day, after a whole afternoon of few customers coming into the store and his watching them pass by in front of the window, Delbert came home, stormed through the door of the house, and shouted, "Jessee! I want to talk to you!"

Jessee appeared at once, frightened by the sound of Delbert's voice. "What is it, honeybee?" she asked, looking up at her husband with her eyes wide and her eyelashes fluttering.

Delbert charged into the kitchen and poured himself a cup of coffee. Jessee followed, twisting her hands nervously, knowing something was terribly wrong.

Delbert turned from the stove. "Business is falling off!" he said in a hard, stony voice. He took a quick gulp of the coffee and Jessee cringed, feeling what must be coming. "I'll put it to you this way, Jessee. If that old boy don't leave, I'll have to!"

"But I told you, honey bear, Daisy ain't no boy!" Jessee tried to keep her voice from shaking, tried to keep it soft and girlish and cute, the way she knew was most appealing, but her whole insides quaked so that even her teeth were chattering.

"I know what you told me!" Delbert said and took another gulp of the coffee. "But what you told me and the way Daisy looks don't match up. The whole durned town is bellering about it."

Jessee began to wring her hands and bite into her lips to keep from crying. What was she going to do? Would she have to go away with Daisy? It seemed too much for her to think about, too hard for her to think about. Oh, if only Mama hadn't died, she thought, and her heart spun in pain for Daisy.

But, somehow, in a way she could not help, the pain she felt for Daisy was not as great as the pain she felt for herself. What would she do out in the world all alone with Daisy to take care of? Where would they go? Where would they live? Her mind raced angrily to the days when she lived in a hovel listening to the rats scratch inside the walls all the night through, having no money and going day after day to that

· 24 ·

greasy café where she stood over steaming pots that made the sweat crawl in her hair, where she carried big trays of food to loud, vulgar men, and where she cleaned the tables and swept the floors and washed the dishes until her life became only that. The pain of it all squeezed her heart so tightly she could hardly breathe. Finally, in a trembling voice, she asked, "Where can Daisy go?"

"Well," Delbert said thoughtfully, "I know, you being Daisy's mama and all, that you wouldn't want to send her out alone." He took another gulp of coffee.

"No . . . no, I wouldn't!" Jessee said quickly with her heart drumming against her pain and her eyes swallowing up the look on Delbert's face.

"How old is Daisy?" Delbert asked.

"Thirteen," Jessee answered, wondering what Delbert had in his mind.

"That's old enough to get hitched," he said. "Lots of girls I know of gets hitched at Daisy's age. Even younger."

Jessee forced back the heavy lump that had formed in her throat as her eyes grew big as moons in her head. "Who is around for Daisy to hitch with?" she managed to ask.

Delbert scratched his chin and the back of his neck and took another drink of coffee. "Ain't no one around here I know of who would have her," he said. "But I heard tell of a man once that put an advertisement in a newspaper over in the city and got him a wife that way."

"A stranger?" Jessee breathed in horror, studying Delbert's face.

"You got a better idea?" Delbert snapped and turned to set his empty coffee cup in the sink.

"Daisy can't marry no stranger, honey bear! She just ain't cut out to marry up with a rank stranger!"

"You know anyone around here who'd have her?" Delbert repeated sharply.

"Daisy can't marry no stranger from the newspaper! Oh, please, please say you won't put no ad in the newspaper, honeybee!" Jessee pleaded as she rushed to Delbert and threw her head against his chest.

Delbert patted her platinum hair and smoothed it down. "What else can we do, Jessee?"

"Ain't there some other way, honey bear?" Delbert sighed deeply and shook his head. Suddenly Jessee's face brightened.

"Maybe you could make a sign and put it in the store winder! That way, everyone in town would see it and maybe . . . maybe some young feller right here in town would be interested. Why, they is no telling how many local boys would want to marry Daisy!"

"A feller would have to be paid a purty penny to hitch up with that gal," Delbert said with a snort.

After a little more conversation, it was decided that Delbert would paint a sign and offer ten dollars to any man or boy who would be willing to marry Daisy Flowerdew.

When Jessee saw the sign, she frowned deeply, "Ten dollars, honey bear?" she asked Delbert.

"Who'd pay more than ten dollars for Daisy?" Delbert said.

"Just don't seem right somehow to *sell* Daisy," Jessee said.

"It ain't *selling* Daisy," Delbert said quickly. "It's just giving a feller a little money to get started on is all. Every young couple needs a little extry money to start out on."

"Oh," Jessee murmured, pressing her hand against her cheek.

Chapter
Four

As soon as Elmer Goots from out south of town opened his mouth about the sign in the store window, Delbert came around from behind the counter with a big grin on his face, grabbed Elmer's hand, and began pumping it up and down.

"You got yourself a deal, boy!"

"Do I get the ten dollars?" Elmer asked eagerly.

"You got to wait till you down right marry Daisy. You got to actual have a wedding ceremony first," Delbert answered.

Elmer frowned, said a disappointed "Oh," and pulled his hand out of Delbert's. "That Daisy as scugugly as I heard tell she is?"

"Oh, Daisy's a fine gal," Delbert said, speaking quickly. "She don't say nothing, don't speak a word, so she won't never talk back at you ner sass you like some women do their men." Delbert hurried on, fearful that Elmer was getting ready to back out of the proposition. "And she sweeps the floors, washes the dishes, makes the beds, even scrubs the front porch off, right down on her hands and knees. They ain't no one better at keeping house than Daisy. She'll make you a good wife. Here!" he went on, dashing behind the counter and forking a fat, briney pickle out of a huge, round glass jar on the counter, "have this tasty pickle to sign the deal on." He held the green, dripping pickle across the counter to Elmer.

"Is it free?" Elmer asked, giving the pickle a suspicious look.

"Why, sure it's free," Delbert said, laughing nervously. "You marry my wife's girl and there'll be lots of free things here for you."

"Like what?" Elmer asked, crunching down on the tangy pickle and relishing the taste of it in his dry mouth.

"Well . . . well. . . ," Delbert stuttered as he skirted his eyes over the bolts of cotton fabric on the shelf along the wall, the stack of canned goods and boxes of soap flakes, and the jaw breakers and other candy in the glass counter case. "Well . . . er . . . just about anything you'd have a mind to have, boy."

"I like a lot of things," Elmer said, chewing so fast that the pickle was already more than half eaten.

"Well . . . you can *have* lots of things!" Delbert told him, feeling more than a little annoyed.

Elmer eyed a pocketknife in one corner of the counter case. It was small and black and heavy-looking with an oval picture of a red quail on it. Delbert followed Elmer's eyes to the pocketknife. "Anything you want in the way of *food*," he said distinctly as he watched Elmer staring at the knife with envy.

"Well, I ain't hungry," Elmer said just as distinctly.

Delbert felt his face turn warm as anger swelled up inside him. "After you're married to Daisy, we can make a few little deals here and there," he told Elmer.

"What kind of deals?" Elmer asked, wiping his wet fingers on his shirt and swallowing the last of the pickle.

"Deals that don't always include food," Delbert snapped, beginning to feel Elmer wasn't as dumb as he looked.

"Don't include food, huh?" Elmer asked, glancing at the pocketknife again.

"You want that ten dollars or not?" Delbert asked sharply. "A feller can do a lot on ten dollars. Why, I bet you ain't even got ten cents in your pocket right now."

"I ain't even got enough money to pay my way to the edge of town, if you want to know the truth," Elmer admitted with a snicker and a swipe of his flannel shirtsleeve across his mouth.

"A ten-dollar bill sure can make a man feel like a million," Delbert went on with a wink.

"You can say that again," Elmer agreed.

"A ten-dollar bill can change—" Delbert started and Elmer cut him off.

"Where's that gal at?" he asked, feeling suddenly convinced that all it would take to make him feel like he owned the world would be that ten dollars he would get for marrying Daisy Flowerdew.

Delbert relaxed and smiled. Now he and Jessee could be alone again, he thought. They could turn on the radio and listen to all them fine T. Texas Tyler songs and spoon on the porch like they used to do before Daisy came. He could even flounce around the house in his underwear if he was a mind to.

After giving Elmer the directions out to his place on Dogtown Road, he reached for the long, thin freckled hand again and, grinning broadly, pumped it up and down. "You won't be sorry, boy. No sir, you won't never be sorry!"

Elmer went to the door, turned, and gave the pocketknife in the counter case one last longing look before he opened the door and walked out.

Chapter Five

"Daisy Flowerdew is a crackbrain!" Olive Goots shouted at her red-headed son when he announced he intended to pay a visit to Daisy.

"Ah, Ma. . . ," Elmer said, making a face. "Daisy can't be that bad."

"She's got herself into a fix, I'll vow! And that mama of hers, that white-haired Jessee, all she wants is to get her off her hands. Ain't a feller around these parts who'd marry that lamebrain-looking thing!" Olive's voice shook and her hands trembled as she shouted up at Elmer. He was four heads taller than her and, now he was seventeen, she knew she couldn't hold him back from doing anything he set his mind to.

"Heck, I like young'uns," Elmer said with a grin.

"You ain't taking on no other man's young'un!" Olive blasted with a final sounding smack of her lips.

"Ah, Ma, Daisy ain't in no fix. Old man Heath is the one in a fix. He's dying to get rid of Daisy so's he can be alone with that purty wife of his," Elmer said and turned to look into the dirty, cracked mirror that hung over the ancient highboy dresser that sat against the cobwebby wall.

Elmer's hair matched his freckles. They were both red.

"How long you going to pretend at the fool, Elmer Goots?" Olive demanded.

Elmer grinned at his reflection in the mirror. "I ain't pretending, Ma," he said.

"They ain't a feller on this planet would have the likes of that Daisy! She's got a brick missing in her chimley and, besides that, she don't look right." It wasn't often that Olive Goots, being a good Christian woman, spoke ill of another human being but, today, with her only son acting up the way he was, she couldn't contain herself.

She shook her head and poked a thin finger into her cheek as she watched him. He hadn't combed that clump of red hair in a coon's age and now, here he was, scraping that old half-toothless comb through it and spiffing up for that strange lump of a girl like she was one of them uppity Howard girls that lived up on the hill above town in that old decaying mansion. Now, Olive thought, pursing her small, narrow lips up tight and leaning her head to the side, as she observed her son's long, lean back and the breadth of his narrow shoulders, if Elmer was to go primping like a peacock to visit them Howard girls, it wouldn't flame up her temper one bit. They was no spring chickens, but what they lost in age they made up for in other ways.

She smacked her mouth again and sent her tongue out to lick her lips and said, "Elmer, why do you want to waste your time with baggage such as that Daisy Flowerdew when you could be getting acquainted with the Howard sisters? Seems to me a fine, good-looking boy like you would prefer the company of them nice book-learned girls to a peabrain like Daisy."

Elmer flipped the comb on the highboy with a loud clatter and turned to grin at his mother. "I ain't had no offer of ten dollars to go and visit them Howard girls, Ma," he said.

"You ain't been offered ten dollars to visit that Daisy, neither! You been offered ten dollars to *marry* her! That's a horse of a whole different color!"

"I got to go see her before I can marry her, don't I?" Elmer asked, still grinning.

Olive mashed her lips down hard against each other and sighed disgustedly. It was a good thing she had only the one young'un to raise, she thought. Two would have done her in. Elmer's father being dead had given her ten long years with the boy. She'd done the best she could by him. But she wondered, narrowing her eyes over Elmer, if she had done good enough. The boy was lazy, had lost every job he ever had, wouldn't work weeks at a time. He was a sight, all right. Too lazy to even sweep out a barn.

Elmer raised his brogan to balance against the edge of a chair seat and spit on it. Then he moved his arm down and rubbed the long sleeve of his flannel shirt across it to give it a shine. He did this with the other brogan while Olive watched in helpless agitation.

"Well, Ma, how do I look?" Elmer asked as he stood up tall and straight and grinned from ear to ear.

"Like a durned little fool that don't know which way the wind blows and his nose right in it!" Olive answered.

"Aw, Ma. . . ," Elmer groaned as he turned and headed out the front door. He crossed the slanting, rotted wood porch, went down the squeaky steps, and swaggered across the muddy yard and down the road, his red hair gleaming brilliantly in the early-morning sun.

From the doorway of the shack, Olive yelled out, "You'll be the joke of the whole durned county, you little fool! Ain't nobody will give you rest if you marry that peabrain Daisy!"

Elmer continued down the road, hearing his mother shout but ignoring her. His mind was on Daisy and the anticipation of meeting her. He clopped along in the mud puddles that the heavy spring rain of the night before had left, caring little that the mud leaped from the road onto his pants and soon dried there in little round cakes. He had to pass through a wide meadow that was damp and soft and caved in under his heavy brogans as he walked. By the time he reached Dogtown Road, wisps of yellow goldenrod and stray daffodils clung to his pant legs and in the loops of his shoelaces.

Dogtown Road, where Delbert Heath's house was,

stretched out long and narrow before Elmer. There was nothing of much interest on either side. Occasionally a scrawny cow or a feeble-looking bull grazed in a pasture and, from time to time, he walked past dilapidated old shacks and lopsided barns with rotting roofs that looked as though they would topple over at any time. In some of the yards he passed, dirty children in baggy diapers played in the mud holes and old folks rocked monotonously on leaning porches.

"I ought to be paid ten dollars just for this durned walk!" Elmer grumbled as he trudged along, swinging his arms and kicking out one leg, then the other in front of him and feeling the first flush of tiredness wash over him. "Bad as old man Heath wants to get her married off, he might fork over an extry ten." He'd have to have a talk with him, he decided. "Shoot fire and save the matches! I never reckoned on it being this far!"

For a long time Elmer clumped along in step with the sound of a whippoorwill high up in a tree near the road. After a while the sound of hunting dogs off in the distance made him quicken his walk. Soon he approached a fence where tangles of honeysuckle grew wildly, looping in and out of the wood slats. The fragrance caught in his nostrils and he sniffed deeply, while throwing his head back to the sky. Behind the fence and back a way was Delbert Heath's house. It was built out of clapboard and had a porch that ran the length of the house. Below the porch were clusters of spring flowers. Elmer stopped, surveyed the fence carefully for a moment, then quickly leaped over it and landed feet first in the yard.

Inside the house, sweeping the front room, Daisy looked out the window just as Elmer came flying across the fence. She glanced at Jessee, setting in a chair beside the radio, then took off in a sudden run to her back-porch room.

"Old man Heath must be doing purty good to have a place like this," Elmer muttered to himself as he went up the steps of the house and lumbered loudly across the porch to the front door. He could hear Hank Snow singing and playing his guitar on the radio from inside the house. He leaned his ear close to the door to listen for a second, then raised his freckled hand to rap loudly on it. He waited several minutes, then rapped harder and, abruptly, the music stopped and he heard footsteps crossing the floor inside the house, nearing the door. When the door opened he yanked his head back and grinned into Jessee Heath's pretty face.

"How do, Miz Heath. I come to gander at that girl of yourn, that Daisy Flowerdew," he said pleasantly.

"Oh!" Jessee exclaimed in a startled way as she stared up into the freckled face that was perched on a long thin neck and an even thinner frame.

"Don't you remember me? I'm Chester and Olive Goots's boy, Elmer."

"Oh . . . Elmer. Oh, why sure, I remember you. Looks like you growed up so much you don't hardly look like yourself."

Elmer snickered. "I'm seventeen and nigh onto six

feet tall," he said proudly and raised his narrow shoulders back and puffed his chest out.

"Well, ain't that nice," Jessee said and she held the door open for Elmer to enter the house.

"Where's this here girl of yourn?" he asked as he glanced around the room, taking in the new-looking blue davenport and matching chair with a smoke stand beside it. There were sheer white curtains at the windows that hung all the way to the floor and pictures hanging on the walls and a small radio setting atop a table that was covered by a white lacy-looking cloth. Elmer had never seen the like of such things. "Where'd you get all this stuff?" he couldn't keep from asking Jessee as she smiled with pride.

"It all come right out of Chicago from the Sears and Roebuck catalogue," she answered.

"Even them pitchers and that there radio?" Elmer could hardly believe it.

Jessee nodded. "My husband, Delbert, has to have the best."

Elmer chuckled and shook his head and immediately thought that if Delbert Heath could afford all this, he surely could afford an extra ten dollars. He studied Jessee's face. She was right pretty, he thought, with cool-looking peachy-colored skin and clear blue eyes, a smile that made his temples thump, and hair so white it looked like the color of pure cotton, still in the bolls, shining in the noonday sun. But he never would have said she was the "best" of anything. He'd heard tell how old man Heath had married Jessee right out of a fast dive over in Hoosier City.

Jessee, noticing how Elmer was staring at her and the slack grin on his face, said quickly, "I'll call Daisy for you."

Elmer listened to the clear, almost musical tone in Jessee's voice as she called Daisy's name. Her voice was almost as pretty as she was, he thought. When there was no response, Jessee called again, a little louder this time. "I don't know why she don't come," she said with a frown knitting her eyebrows together. She went into the kitchen and pushed open the door that led to the back porch. Elmer followed her.

"Daisy?" Jessee questioned the air as her eyes sped all around the vacant room. She went to the cot where the blankets were all piled up and yanked them back with a swift, angry thrust. "Daisy!" she shouted and Elmer was surprised at the sudden coarseness in Jessee's voice. It was as if the music in it had died.

Jessee, looking angry and frustrated, rushed to the window that looked out over the wide expanse of land that fled away from the house into the woods. "I reckon she ain't here," she said wearily as she turned around and faced Elmer.

"How come she ain't here?" Elmer asked in an agitated voice.

"Well, I don't know. She was here. Just a few minutes ago." Jessee looked worried.

"You mean to tell me I come all the way out here and that girl of yourn ain't here?" Elmer was so disgusted he felt like turning around and marching right out of that house without saying another word to Jessee. But the memory of Delbert Heath's ten dollars was like a picture in his mind, all green and crisp with the number "ten" flashing out at him like the lights in the juke boxes he'd seen in the honky-tonk dives over in Hoozier City. He could even hear the quick, foot-stomping music.

"I'll go outside and call for her," Jessee said nervously. "Sometimes she goes down by Toby's Creek."

"How come she goes into the woods?" Elmer asked, thinking it was strange that a girl would go and hang around the woods all alone. But then he remembered the town talk about how strange Daisy was and he decided that anything she might do would probably be strange too.

"Well, I don't know why," Jessee answered. "Daisy is kind of attached to the birds and things, I reckon."

Attached to birds and things! If it hadn't been for the ten dollars still making music in his brain, Elmer would have stomped away right then and there. Besides, wasn't no girl he knew of worth hanging around and waiting till darkness fell, making him have to walk all the way back to his place in the moonlight!

Jessee headed out of the house and Elmer followed close at her heels, noticing with a grin how slim her ankles were in a pair of backless house slippers. They walked to the back of the house, where there was a good view of the lush trees and foliage where the woods began and where Toby's Creek snaked through the shadowy dimness. Jessee's voice rang out across the woods, calling Daisy's name repeatedly. The only answer that came was the sound of a whippoorwill in a high tree. Daisy did not appear.

"I reckon you'll have to come back tomorrow," Jessee said finally, her voice sounding dispirited and weary.

"Tomorrow!" Elmer exploded.

"I'll have Daisy here for sure," Jessee promised, looking worriedly into Elmer's angry face.

Without another word, Elmer whipped around and beat an angry path across the front yard, leaped over the slat fence, and charged down the road snarling and cursing to himself. "Ain't no gal worth having to come back to see way out here!" he barked to the road. "Not even for ten whole durned dollars!"

Chapter Six

Daisy lay in the deep grass on the bank of Toby's Creek, gazing up into the heavy, dangling leaves of the overhead trees and thinking about Granny Henry, who was all the way over in Punkin Center in her grave. It seemed such a short time ago to her when Granny Henry took sick and lay in her bed close to death. When she still had the energy she had called Daisy to her bedside and told her to listen to what she had to say.

"Bend down low, child, so's you can hear good," Granny Henry told her and as she leaned over the small little lump of quilt that was Granny, Granny Henry placed her thin wrinkled hands on each side of Daisy's face and looked deeply into her eyes. "You ain't normal in your looks, child. And you don't talk to folks. You talk to posies and birds and trees and such. If you was normal, you'd talk to folks and smile and greet them like is expected of you." Granny Henry stopped and sighed like she was trying to gather all her breath to say what she had to say. "Being taunted and teased all your life has made you fearful of folks. But, the Lord knows, you wouldn't be afraid if folks had treated you right." Granny Henry stopped and sighed again and Daisy felt the sting of tears behind her eyes. "But folks is ignorant, Daisy. They don't know much of how to treat another human unless they look and act like they do. So you've been left out of all the joys of life and been mistreated until you don't know how to act." Granny Henry stopped again, catching her breath, then went on slowly. "Your ma didn't know how to treat you neither, and your pa, he ain't been around ever since you was borned. He was a reckless, aimless, wandering feller with nary a responsible bone in his body."

Granny Henry's words disappeared into a rattling cough; when she was able to, she went on in a shaking voice. "Folks say you're teched and call you fierce names, but I know you understand what they're saying. You've knowed things all your life about human nature, just like I have." The cough came again. "I've learned you to read and you've read them books we got here in the house over and over to yourself. Them books by Longfellow and Whitman and the rest. I've seen the pleasure in your face whilst your eyes run over the words. You're smarter than most in my estimation, Daisy Flowerdew, but you ain't normal in the ways folks expects you to be."

Suddenly Granny Henry's words sounded as though they were being torn right out of her chest and her eyes widened. "When I'm gone, you'll have an even harder time getting by in this old life. I won't be here to watch out for you. You'll have to protect yourself, Daisy." Granny Henry's lips started to tremble and her old, gray eyes filled with tears. She clutched the sides of Daisy's face so hard that Daisy felt pain shoot through her jaws. "You got feet as swift as a terrified deer running from the gun, Daisy. And that's what you'll have to use! Run! Run away if you feel trapped and can't find no other way out. Run as fast as you can when you feel in harm's way!"

Daisy felt tears splash out of her eyes and settle in her eyelashes as Granny Henry's hands shook her face hard. "Run, Daisy!" Daisy felt Granny Henry's hands slip suddenly away from her cheeks and she watched in horror as the old woman fell back into her pillow and closed her eyes.

Daisy leaned low over Granny Henry and kissed her forehead and her cheeks and the tops of her old blotchy-colored hands. Then she folded the hands under the quilt and tucked it close around Granny Henry's neck. She knew Granny Henry wasn't dead. But she could hear the short, feeble breaths that Granny Henry seemed to struggle for and she realized death was not far away. She climbed on the bed and lay beside the old woman for a long, long time, until Aunt Lou came into the room and told her to get up, that she couldn't keep Granny Henry from dying.

Granny Henry died that very afternoon and it

wasn't more than a few minutes after the quilt was drawn over her face that Uncle Flint gave Daisy a pained look and said, "You'll have to go to your ma's over in Vineyard Flats. Ain't no way me and Lou can take care of you and ain't no one in Punkin Center can take care of you neither."

Daisy had looked right into Uncle Flint's dark eyes without even blinking. "I wish there was some way . . . but they ain't, Daisy. They just ain't no way," he went on. Daisy forced herself to look away from Uncle Flint; she gazed down at her feet and at the floor where the rag rug lay that she had helped Granny Henry make. It had been washed and sewn together so much after years of walking on that it was full of frays and loose threads. The colors were faded too, and looking at it made Daisy want to be alone, to lie down on the rag rug and cry because she missed Granny Henry so much already.

"Me and Lou will take you to your ma's place this afternoon. She's got herself a new husband, but I reckon she'll just have to make room for you," Uncle Flint said and then he hurried away, out of the bedroom.

"My real ma," Daisy whispered to the quilt that covered Granny Henry on the bed. "You was my real ma, Granny," she said and she went to the bed and knelt down and tried to think of all the things she wanted to say to Granny Henry that she could never say before. Things like thanking her for taking her in and caring for her and loving her and giving her books to read and songs to sing inside her heart. And for protecting her. She wished she could thank her for the way she always sang and hummed hymns and the way she laughed and slapped her skinny knee sometimes when she thought Daisy wasn't paying any attention to her. "Child, I'm just setting here talking to hear my old head rattle," she would say and they both would laugh. There would be no laughter now, Daisy realized as she raised up and patted all the wrinkles out of the quilt. She went to the window beside Granny Henry's bed and looked out.

"I'm going to my real ma's house," she whispered to the sweet peas that grew along the side of the house and climbed up a string all the way to the window. "But she ain't my real ma," she said fiercely. She looked back at the lump of Granny Henry, then at the little book of poetry that lay on the bedside table. It was always there waiting for Granny to open it up and read from it. Daisy went to the little book and touched it gently with her fingers. The cover was faded and the pages discolored. But the printed words were still bright and easy to read. Daisy opened the book. "Somewhere in the darkness and mist, the winter flowers were kissed. . . ." She formed the words into a silent whisper, closed the book, and continued the poem in her mind with her eyes closed and tears trickling down her cheeks.

After a while Aunt Lou came back into the room and told Daisy to put all her things into a box. Then she came to her and touched her hair and looked sad. "I'm sorry, Daisy. Ma would of wanted you to stay here forever, but we just can't take care of you the way she done. It's time you was with your real ma now."

Daisy turned to look at Granny Henry on the bed under the quilt one last time before she walked out of the room. It was a good-bye look and a thank-you look and a look of love that said how much she would miss Granny Henry.

Daisy turned over in the deep mossy grass and nestled her cheek into the long, soft blades, remembering how Uncle Flint and Aunt Lou had driven her all the way to Vineyard Flats in the Model A Ford with her setting in the back in the rumble seat, stiff and straight, her box of clothes in her lap. She remembered how the wind had blown through her hair and how there had been no sound on the long, narrow road except for Uncle Flint and Aunt Lou talking and talking.

"Jessee will be as mad as a hornet when she sees us pull up with Daisy," Aunt Lou said in a low voice, but her words were carried on the wind and Daisy heard them.

For a long time Aunt Lou and Uncle Flint were quiet and there was no other sound but the car monotonously sputter-chugging along the dusty road. Daisy got lost in the sound and in her mind the sputter-chug . . . sputter-chug . . . sputter-chug sounded like wheels turning over and over saying, "Granny Henry is dead . . . sputter-chug . . . Granny Henry is dead . . . sputter-chug. . . ." Then, suddenly, the wheels stopped and Uncle Flint was saying in a truculent voice, "Jessee thinks she's so highfalutin with her marrying that Heath feller and him owning that dry goods store!"

"Jessee's got above her raising, that's what she's done," Aunt Lou said with a quiet sniff.

"She'll topple right over into being her own true self when she sees that we've brought Daisy to her," Uncle Flint said and he glanced back to the rumble seat.

Daisy looked down at the old rumpled shirt in the top of the box. "She give me to Granny Henry because she didn't want me," she said in her mind. She looked from the shirt into the trees they passed that grew at the side of the road. Birds twittered and made the leaves move. She got tears in her eyes thinking about how quickly after the funeral they had left and how she hadn't even had a chance to look at the house or the garden one last time or to get a picture of Granny Henry to keep. But, she had managed to quickly sneak the book of poems from Granny Henry's night table down into the deepest part of the box under her clothes before Uncle Flint had snapped the box up and started carrying it out of the house.

Daisy pushed her hand down into the box and found the spine of the book and held it tightly, as though it were Granny Henry's hand reaching out to her. She could remember every poem in it. And, as the car sputter-chugged along, and the intermittent sound of Uncle Flint and Aunt Lou's talking mixed in with it, she began to say each poem in her mind, be-

ginning with the very first poem in the book and ending with the very last one. She knew them all by heart
and, by the time she said the last one, the car had
stopped in front of a pleasant-looking house with a
wide porch that was behind a white fence that had
pretty-smelling honeysuckle winding all through it.
Daisy's heart began to thunder and she gripped the
spine of the book even harder.

"Well, here we are," Uncle Flint said as he surveyed the house with his dark, critical eyes.

"Looks like Jessee married herself a man with property," Aunt Lou said.

"You can get out now, Daisy," Uncle Flint said,
turning to give Daisy a tender-hearted look. He and
Aunt Lou got out of the car and Daisy quickly pulled
her hand out of the box. Uncle Flint came toward
her. "Come on now, Daisy," he urged her and she
stood up. But before she jumped down to the
ground, her eyes were drawn to a figure just coming
out the front door of the house.

"Daisy?" Uncle Flint's voice called again.

When Daisy's feet hit the ground, she saw that the
figure coming out of the house was a woman. A very
pretty woman with snow-white hair and eyes the
color of the clearest blue sky. She wore a thin, gauzy-
looking print dress and an expression of shock and
surprise on her face. The woman's eyes fled back
and forth from Uncle Flint and Aunt Lou to Daisy,
and then she moved to the edge of the porch and
wrapped an arm around one of the posts as though
she wished it to steady her.

Daisy knew the woman must be her mother and her heart seemed to stop and start again, over and over, until she thought she would fall over from the dizziness.

Daisy squeezed hard at the handful of grass as she remembered that first meeting and recalled the look of horror on Jessee's face when she realized who Uncle Flint and Aunt Lou had brought with them that day.

Chapter Seven

"What y'all doing here?" Jessee called out in an uncertain voice while her eyes continued to flit like a nervous butterfly across the three faces. But then they lighted for a long time on Daisy, studying her dark overalls and flannel shirt, the clumpy brogans and her peculiar face.

"Ma passed on. We've brought your girl to you," Uncle Flint answered Jessee. "We call her Daisy Flowerdew."

"Oh, Ma!" Jessee cried. "I should of gone to see her!"

"It's too late now, Jessee," Uncle Flint said. "We done buried her."

Jessee made a thick whimpering sound and rubbed a hand across her mouth. Daisy watched her curiously.

"There weren't no way we could keep care of Daisy, Jessee," Aunt Lou went on with a worried frown on her face. "She's yourn and it's time you took her. Daisy knows a lot of things. She ain't dumb. She's just, well, she don't say nothing . . . but she understands all right." When she finished, her voice was shaking. She looked from Jessee to Daisy and back again.

"Her clothes is right here," Uncle Flint said and he started carrying the box to the porch where Jessee stood.

As Uncle Flint walked, the small book of poems somehow worked its way up out of the box and went tumbling to the ground. Daisy felt herself fill with panic as Aunt Lou leaned down to pick it up and exclaimed, "Looky here, Flint, it's Ma's poetry book!"

Uncle Flint turned and stared at the book in Aunt Lou's hand. "Now how did that get in with Daisy's things?"

"I always liked this poetry book, Flint. It belongs on Ma's night table," Aunt Lou said and she dusted the book off against her skirt, opened her pocketbook, and dropped the small book into it.

Even now, lying in the grass, far away from that day, Daisy could feel the same deep sense of loss as she had when she watched Aunt Lou slip the book of poems into her purse. Granny Henry was gone and the book, the only thing she had of Granny Henry, was gone too. And, as though it were real in that very moment, she could still hear the angry, sick sound of

Jessee's voice calling out that day as though she were a child alone and afraid, "What am I supposed to do with Daisy?"

Daisy stared at Jessee, watching how she twisted her hands, how her whole pretty face seemed to crumple up like she was going to cry. I don't know *how* to take care of . . . of a girl like Daisy!" she whimpered.

"Aw, now, Jessee," Uncle Flint said, looking up at Jessee after setting the box of clothes on the porch. "Ain't no reason to go to crying. Daisy can take care of herself mostly. Matter of fact, she was right smart to help Ma out. Anyways, she stays to herself most of the time."

"Come up here, Daisy!" Uncle Flint called to her but Daisy didn't move.

"Go to your mama, Daisy," Aunt Lou said and she came close to Daisy and patted her shoulder. "You got to go up there and meet your mama," she whispered, and Daisy took a deep breath and began walking slowly toward the porch.

Uncle Flint started walking back toward the car. Behind her, as she walked, Daisy heard the car start up, heard it begin to chug away, and her heart pounded with fear.

Suddenly Jessee ran to the edge of the porch and yelled to the disappearing car, "*What* am I going to *do* with *Daisy*?"

The car kept going, chugging and sputtering, until its sound was lost in the trees and the sky. Daisy stared at her mother, watching the tears streaming down Jessee's cheeks. When the car was out of sight, Jessee slumped down on the step and dropped her head into her hands and cried as though she would never stop. The forlorn sound filled the whole world, Daisy thought. It made her feel helpless and weak, as though she couldn't stand it a minute longer. It made her want to run! To run away just like Granny Henry told her to, when she felt frightened and in harm's way. But where, she wondered, could she run to in this strange new place.

After a little, Jessee raised her head and lifted the hem of her dress and wiped it over her eyes. "Y-you j-just better n-not give me no trouble, Daisy Flowerdew," she said in a hard, even voice without even looking at Daisy. *"You just better not!"*

Daisy turned in the grass and lay on her stomach for a long time with the memory of Jessee's words throbbing in her temples. She knew she was giving Jessee trouble right now, this very minute. Jessee had been calling and calling her name, her voice traveling over the grass and up through the trees and swirling all around her, but she would not get up and run to the house. *She would not.* She knew there was a stranger there. A tall red-haired man. Someone who, like the ladies who had come to meet her that other day, only wanted to stare at her, study her, and make her feel bad.

Jessee continued to call until the sound of her voice was like a drum in Daisy's ears. After a while, she covered her ears with her hands and Jessee's voice went away.

Chapter
Eight

Elmer Goots headed straight for town. His feet kept moving at a hard, swift pace until he reached Main Street, where Heath's Dry Goods Store was. He hung around in front until all the customers straggled out, then he hurried inside and went directly to the counter, where Delbert was calculating some figures in a long, narrow book with lines on the pages. He placed his hands on the glass-topped counter and Delbert looked up. Seeing the look of extreme agitation on Elmer's face, Delbert's heart began to pump and pound with the fear that Elmer had come to tell him he'd changed his mind about marrying Daisy after seeing her.

"Well?" Delbert managed to say from his dry, nervous throat.

"She weren't there," Elmer said flatly and Delbert

felt a rush of relieved air course through his lungs. But he felt agitated, too.

"How come she weren't there?" he asked, glaring at Elmer.

"How should I know? Her ma, your wife, she said for me to come back tomorrow. I don't know so much about that. . . ."

Delbert set his pencil down and closed the book. "What do you mean, you 'don't know so much about that'? Ain't you still innerested?" Delbert's heart began to pound again. Deep inside he knew that Elmer Goots was his only chance to get rid of Daisy.

Elmer scratched his freckled cheek and shifted his weight from one leg to the other. "Well . . . the thing about it is, it's so durn far out to your place, past meadows and pastures and, heck, a feller could die of heat stroke before he even got there. And . . ."

"Aw," Delbert said, coming from around the counter and leaning on the glass case, "it ain't that far. A young feller like you, why you ought to be able to walk six miles in nothing flat. You ought to be able to walk farther than that in one whip and not get worn out."

"It's *twelve* miles round trip," Elmer said. Then he looked down at his worn-out brogans with the loose soles and raised one up. "These here boots is as heavy as any man can stand to walk in. They has near about seen their last walking days. Fact of the matter is, I don't believe I can walk out to your place again unless I have me some boots that is light on my feet." Elmer forgot about the extra ten dollars he had planned to ask Delbert for as his eyes lit on a pair of dandy-looking boots that stood against the wall on a low shelf. The boots were deep brown in color and the toes shone just like they had been recently polished. They had long laces that looked like they never would break. You could even tie them twice, they were so long.

Delbert's eyes flashed to the wall where the best pair of shoes in the whole store sat. "You don't mean *them*?" He looked back at Elmer.

"Yes, sir. I could walk to the end of the county line and back a thousand times in them fine boots," Elmer said enthusiastically as he went to the shelf and picked up one of the boots and stood admiring it, turning it over and over in his big, thin hands.

Delbert dashed to the shelf and took the boot out of Elmer's hand. "You couldn't afford these boots, boy," he said as he set the boot neatly back on the shelf next to its mate.

"Well, I was just thinking. . . ," Elmer said and he lowered his head and scratched at his chin.

"Thinking what?" Delbert asked, narrowing his eyes at Elmer and that mop of red hair.

Elmer looked up. "If you want me to go back out to see that girl you're trying to get married off, you'll have to lend me them boots. I ain't going to ruin my feet going out there no more in these old pieces of cardboard." He raised one leg and dangled his foot in the air. "It's them boots or nothing."

Delbert narrowed his eyes even more at Elmer. "What do you take me for? Them boots is priced at fifteen dollars."

"Ain't no one going to buy them boots," Elmer said matter-of-factly. "I seen them same boots setting here a whole year ago. No one wants new boots they has to break in and pay that much money for. They want easy walking, broke-in boots like they can get at Miz Minnie's barn sale."

Delbert studied the boots with a heavy frown. Well, the truth of the matter was, he thought, those boots had been setting there on the shelf for over a year and been passed over by every man and boy in town. Maybe Elmer had a point. If Elmer could break in the boots, Delbert would be willing to bring the price down a couple of dollars for the wear on them. Maybe someone would be willing to buy them then. He looked up and watched Elmer take both boots off the shelf and inspect them.

"I reckon you got a point in what you say," Delbert admitted.

"Why, sure I have," Elmer said with a flash of delight soaring across his face. He carried the boots over to a chair near the counter, sat down in it, and proceeded to take his boots off and to put the new boots on. He got up and walked back and forth across the floor while Delbert watched him. "They feel like new boots, all right. Hurt like hell fire blazing across my heels. I reckon they need some good breakin in before anyone would want them. If you got a sack, I'll carry my old boots and wear these. They need all the breakin in they can get."

Delbert went behind the counter, got a sack, came back, and very gingerly dropped Elmer's dilapidated boots into it. "You'll have to bring them back right after you get back from my place tomorrow," he said as he shoved the sack into Elmer's hands.

Elmer leaned on the counter with a slack smile on his face. "You being as smart as you are to know that these boots needs to be broke in before you can sell them, I reckon you would know just by your smartness that a feller like me would need a good shirt to wear to go and see that girl of your wife's in." Elmer looked down at his shirt. "Looky here at this place where my ma done patched it. They is a green circle where the rest of the shirt is brown. And looky here . . ." He raised his arm and showed Delbert a long tear at the elbow.

Delbert's eyes flashed with suspicion. He wasn't born yesterday and he wasn't going to let someone like Elmer Goots come along and take advantage of him. "Ain't a thing wrong with that shirt you got on," he said evenly.

"You mean, you'd let a feller that looks as low-down ratty as me go to see that gal you're trying to get married off? Why, I'm glad she wasn't there to-day! Yes, sir, I'm glad Daisy Flowerdew didn't have to get a gander of me looking like the poorest, most pitifulest feller in the whole durned county! To tell you the truth, Mr. Heath, I'm plumb ashamed of myself that I ain't got no decent clothes to go to courting that gal in!" Elmer's face was a crumpled mass of red freckles.

"You don't need to court her! Just marry her!" Delbert almost shouted.

"Why, I ain't never heard of no gal what didn't want a little courting done!" Elmer swiped his sleeve under his nose and took a loud sniff.

Delbert could have sworn the boy was on the verge of crying. "Well, just simmer down a minute," he said with a frown. He had to admit Elmer had a point. It wouldn't look right for the boy to go and ask a girl, even Daisy, to marry him looking like something the dogs had drug up from out of Miz Minnie's trash heap. But, more than that, he couldn't take a chance on Elmer's backing out on asking Daisy to marry him. He went over to a shelf near the shoe shelf and pulled out a plaid shirt with pearl buttons down the front. Elmer's eyes lit up. "Try this on for size," Delbert said, handing the shirt to Elmer.

Elmer laid the sack on the counter, quickly pulled the shirt on, and raised the sleeve to sniff its newness. He smiled at Delbert. "You sure can tell this here is a new shirt, all right," he said. Then his smile turned to a frown as he looked down at his faded trousers, with the round circles of grease near the pockets, where he had wiped his hands, and at the legs of the trousers where ragged strings hung down onto the new boots. Delbert followed his eyes suspiciously.

"Don't seem right—" Elmer started but Delbert cut him off.

"If you think you're going to get a new pair of pants out of me, you've got another think coming!" he blasted.

"You want that gal married off good and proper, don't you? You want her out of your way, don't you, so's you can be alone with that good-looking wife you got, don't you?" Elmer's voice was loud but filled with the truth, Delbert had to admit. He would be a fool to let a chance of getting rid of Daisy slip by. He spun around and walked straight back to the shelf where he had got the shirt and pulled down a pair of denim pants.

"What size do you wear?" he snapped at Elmer.

Elmer laughed joyously to himself. This was getting easier and easier, he thought. "Give me a size twenty-eight waist," he answered.

"You ain't very large," Delbert said as he looked down at the pants to check them for size. They were too large. He put them back on the shelf and began searching for Elmer's size.

"I take after my daddy," Elmer said.

"He was skinny, all right," Delbert agreed.

"But he weren't as tall," Elmer said.

"Well, here's a pair of twenty-eights," Delbert said, turning from the shelf with the pants. "Don't know if they'll fit you in length, though." He took the pants over to Elmer and held them up to his waist. "Too short," he said. "And these is the only twenty-eights I've got."

"I'll take them," Elmer said and he grabbed the pants out of Delbert's hands and shoved them into the sack with the old brogans. "Long as they is new, don't matter if they is a little short."

"Well, I reckon you're all set then," Delbert said with relief. "Just make sure you get them boots back to me as soon as you get back from my place tomorrow. Bring that shirt and them pants back too."

Elmer started toward the door, then stopped.

"They is one more thing I been thinking about," Elmer said and he looked down at the top of the boots where the strings on his pants hung across them.

"What's that?" Delbert asked.

"Ain't it proper for a feller to take a gal some posies when he goes to ask her to hitch up with him?"

"I reckon," Delbert said, remembering the time he had asked Jessee to be his bride and how he had not only taken her a bouquet of flowers but a big box of candy as well. "But it don't matter with Daisy."

Elmer shook his head and rubbed his chin. "I never knowed you was so hard-hearted."

"I ain't hard-hearted!"

"Yes, you are! You want to get that gal off your hands, but you don't want her to get no pleasure out of it!"

Delbert's shoulders sank and his chest caved in. He glared at Elmer for a second, then he hurried behind the counter and banged open the cash register. He pulled out a dollar and handed it across the counter to Elmer. "Here," he said. "Buy Daisy some posies. And don't call me hard-hearted!"

Elmer took the dollar and stared at it.

"Well?" Delbert demanded.

"Well, I been thinking while I been standing here. I been thinking you might as well go ahead on and give me that whole ten dollars now. . . ."

"Now wait a minute!" Delbert exploded. "You don't get that ten dollars until you marry Daisy! That was the deal!"

"I'm sick of that deal! I need money to make it a pleasure for that gal and if I can't make it a pleasure for her, then I ain't going to do it!"

"You backing out on me?" Delbert asked in a low, worried voice. Elmer sniffed, but did not speak. "Now, don't be hasty, boy. Daisy is a fine strapping gal, don't speak a word from morning till night and is as good a cook as you'll ever find. You'd have to look far and wide to meet her match."

"Well . . . I don't know," Elmer hedged. "Without that ten dollars, I can't even buy her a ring."

"Hummm. . . ," Delbert said and he picked up the pencil from the counter and wiggled it back and forth between his fingers. "You for sure and for certain going to marry Daisy?"

"What else would I do after you done give me these fine clothes to meet the gal in and put me to wearing these fine boots to break in for you so's you can sell them and give me that dollar so's I could buy her some posies?" Elmer asked, his eyebrows raised and looking as innocent and as honest as the day is long.

Once again, Delbert thought, Elmer did seem to have a point. It was against his better judgment, but . . . He went behind the counter, opened the cash register, and pulled out a smart, crisp ten-dollar bill. It was the only ten-dollar bill inside the register. Reluctantly, he handed the bill across the counter to Elmer.

Elmer reached out and grabbed it and cried "Hot dog!" He stuffed it into his pants pocket, snapped up the paper sack, and started for the door.

Delbert stopped him. "When you going to see Daisy?"

"Tomorrow. Yes sir, tomorrow."

"You just be sure you don't plan to do nothing else with that money, you hear me, Elmer? And you be back out to my place tomorrow!"

"That gal is as good as hitched!" Elmer tossed across his shoulder as he flew out the door and headed off down the street.

Delbert went to the window and looked out to see if he could tell in what direction Elmer would go when he crossed the street, but Elmer quickly disappeared behind Cooney Rawls's big, broad frame. Cooney was headed toward the store so Delbert rushed back behind the counter and made himself look busy, all the while wondering if he had done the right thing in letting Elmer Goots get away with so much store goods and that ten-dollar bill.

Chapter
Nine

"How do, Elmer," Cooney Rawls said to Elmer as he swept past her rattling a sack in his hand. Elmer didn't answer and it seemed to Cooney that he was in an awful big hurry. In fact, she had never seen the lazy boy move so fast. She just had time to get a quick glance at the new-looking boots and shirt he was wearing as he whizzed past her. Cooney had never seen Elmer wearing anything new. She let out an annoyed "Humph!" and continued on her way into Heath's Dry Goods Store.

Elmer rushed on, ignoring the fat old lady, and when he came to the corner of the street he took a swift turn and tossed the sack around the big, gnarled trunk of a pepper tree in the alley behind Silas Judd's Pool Hall. He knew, if he hung around long enough, he was bound to meet up with one of the old hoboes who hung around in the alley. And it wasn't long before he did.

The Roadrunner turned off the street and headed up the alley toward Elmer, carrying his cooking gear in a heavy canvas bag tied to his back. He walked so fast that his feet hardly seemed to touch the ground. The tin pie plates and cups in his bag clanked together as he hurried along, making a loud racket in the day. The Roadrunner's back was bent from years of carrying the load on his back and he walked with a decided stoop forward, swinging his arms up and down as if, in a way, to balance him and keep him from falling head first into the ground. The old man was never called anything but the Roadrunner, because he walked from town to town, always on the move, never staying in any one place longer than it took to swig down enough booze to fuel him up and move him on to a new town. Elmer watched him with a mixture of amazement and amusement.

When the red, puffy-faced old man reached Elmer, he said a gruff-voiced "Howdy" but did not stop.

"Say," Elmer called out. "I got a favor to ask you."

The Roadrunner stopped and spun around, clanking loudly.

"I'm going to a fancy party up on the hill at the Howards' place and I need to take a bottle of brandy to old man Howard. Wouldn't look right for me to pay a visit and not take something. You reckon you could get it for me? Old man Judd won't sell me nothing. Not even if I was to stand on my head and beg like a dog."

The Roadrunner studied Elmer for a moment, then said, "It'll cost you."

"That don't bother me none," Elmer said. "I got money and plenty of it." He shoved his hand into his pocket and pulled out the ten-dollar bill Delbert Heath had given him and handed it to the Roadrunner.

The Roadrunner took the bill, staring at it with suspicious eyes. "Where'd you get this?" he asked, looking up at Elmer.

"I . . . er . . . well, I worked for it, that's what I done. I even had more than that to buy these here boots and this here shirt I got on," Elmer answered, glancing at the clothes Delbert had loaned him.

The Roadrunner squinted questioning eyes over Elmer for a moment, then turned around and headed across the alley into the back entrance of Silas Judd's Pool Hall.

"Watch that old man Judd gives you back the right change!" Elmer called after him. The Roadrunner did not look back. He whipped across the alley faster than Elmer could count to three, tinking and clattering, with the sun beating hot spots over the tin handles of the skillets that protruded out of the top of the bag on his back.

While the Roadrunner was inside the pool hall, Elmer rushed to take the new pair of pants he had got from Delbert out of the sack. He stood behind the pepper tree and changed into the pants so fast he almost lost his balance and fell. When he finally had them on, he realized that they fit as smooth as a glove. Except for one thing. They were so short they rose up above the tops of the new boots and even showed some of his bare leg. He stuffed the old pair of pants into the sack and gave it a swift toss into the weedy field behind the tree.

By this time the Roadrunner was coming out the door of the pool hall with a small bag in his hand. Elmer popped out from behind the tree and grabbed the bag. The Roadrunner handed him the change from the ten dollars wordlessly. Elmer counted it carefully.

"You took two dollars!" Elmer accused hotly.

"That's what I done," the Roadrunner admitted, squinting narrowly at Elmer.

"Well, that's too much!"

"I done you a favor, didn't I? You know anyone else who'd take that story about you working for that ten dollars without turning you in for stealing it? For two dollars, I ain't asking you nuthin'."

Elmer stuffed the change into his pocket impatiently and yanked the bag off the bottle of brandy to inspect it. "I ain't touched a drop," the Roadrunner said.

"Good thing you didn't," Elmer told him. "I'm saving this for old man Howard and them high-toned daughters of his."

The Roadrunner turned around with a sly smile and walked back across the alley into the pool hall, the bag on his back shuddering and bonging resoundingly.

Elmer glanced around cautiously, then hurriedly opened the bottle of brandy. The old man ought not to mind if he took just one little swig, he thought, as he raised the bottle to his lips and took a sip. Then he stuffed the bottle into the waist of his pants and dropped his shirttail over it. The sweet, fruity taste of the brandy lit up Elmer's brain and made him feel suddenly stronger and more courageous than he had ever thought of being. Now he could go up to that old mansion on the hill and set with the Howard girls without feeling a bit self-conscious or lacking in any way. He raised his arm and ran the sleeve of the new shirt across his mouth, letting it linger under his nose for a moment so that he could smell the newness of it again. Then he shot his long arm into the air and yelled out to the heavens, "YAAAHOOOOOOOO!" and took off walking and whistling toward the road at the edge of town that led up the hill to the mansion where the Howard girls lived.

Chapter Ten

In the afternoon, after Elmer Goots had left, Jessee spied Daisy walking up through the back field behind the house as she was hanging out the wash. Suddenly she was struck by an uncontrollable fury and sent the towel in her hand flying angrily to the ground. Her hands flew to her hips and she shouted, "Daisy Flowerdew, where have you been? I've been calling all day for you! Elmer Goots was here to make your acquaintance and you was nowhere to be seen!"

Daisy approached her mother looking fearfully up through her eyelashes. She wanted to turn and run back into the woods, but somehow she kept walking toward Jessee, against her fear. If only she could make her understand, Daisy thought painfully. If *only* she could make her see that she didn't want to meet the red-haired boy or anyone else. Why couldn't Jessee just leave her alone?

When Daisy reached the clothesline, Jessee reached out and grabbed her arm. "I wish to God you'd open that mouth of yourn and talk! I wish to God I knowed what was going on in that head of yourn. You just missed the chance of meeting your husband-to-be, you little fool. You just better pray that Elmer Goots don't back out because of you acting like such a fool and not coming when I called. Oh, I know you heard me, damn your hide! Now, you get up to that house and wash up them dishes in the sink!"

Jessee gave Daisy a last hard shove and Daisy went stumbling off toward the house. Her mind was in a flurry. In a storm. In a hurricane. "Your husband-to-be," Jessee had said. *Husband-to-be!* The hurricane blew full force into Daisy's heart and plunged down deep into her soul. Husband-to-be! NOOOOO! she cried out from the depths of her. She began to feel as though she would die. If only she could run away! Run away, back to Punkin Center and Granny Henry! Her temples throbbed and her heart pounded and her brain ached as the hurricane blasted all through her insides. She reached the house panting with fear, hearing Jessee shouting behind her. "I don't know what I'm going to do with you, Daisy Flowerdew!"

Yes, you do, Daisy's mind shouted through the wild torrent inside her. You know exactly what you're going to do with me! You're going to try to marry me off to that boy that was here. The one that jumped over the fence! "Oh, Granny, what am I going to do?" she mumbled chokingly as she dashed around the house and up on the front porch.

Inside the kitchen Daisy attacked the sinkful of dishes like some demon power had overtaken her and she was merely a bystander watching her hands in the soapy water. All the while she was thinking about Granny Henry and wondering what she would do if she knew Jessee and Delbert were planning such a thing.

As Daisy was pouring the water out of the dishpan, Jessee came into the house slamming the screen door behind her. Daisy heard her drop into a chair and turn on the radio. Soon music drifted up to the ceiling of the house and sped all around in the rooms. Someone sang to the plink-plank of a guitar and Jessee began to sing too. There was a sweetness in her voice that made Daisy stop still and turn her head to listen. But soon the music stopped and Jessee called out, "I should of follered a band, Daisy. I was good enough to sing with Hank Williams, if I'd wanted to. But . . . I met your daddy and that was that."

My daddy! Daisy thought wonderingly. It was the first time Jessee had mentioned her daddy. My daddy . . . The man Granny Henry had called reckless and aimless and without a responsible bone in his body. She dried her hands and went to the kitchen doorway to listen, hoping to hear more about her father, but Jessee looked up at her with a frown on her face and snapped, "You finished with them dishes? I need you to sweep off the front porch."

Before Daisy could take another breath, someone

knocked on the door. Jessee got a sour look on her face, snapped off the radio, and got up to answer it, pushing her white curls off her face.

"Howdy-do, ma'am," Daisy heard the friendly-sounding voice of a man say to Jessee from the doorway. "I'm Yule Shipton, your paper doll agent out of Stillwater. Work for the McLoughlin Brothers Company."

Daisy edged toward the front window to peer out onto the porch. A man she had never seen before was just tipping his hat to Jessee. He had a broad, pleasant smile on his round face, and even though he was short and appeared to be old, there wasn't a wrinkle on his whole face. He was wearing a dark suit and a stiff-looking white collar that his chin sat in. The collar, like some tall tower, seemed to be holding up his whole head. His dark shoes were covered with powdery sprinkles of dust and he held a small cardboard suitcase in his left hand. He put his hat back on his head and looked down at the suitcase.

"Ma'am, what I carry right here in this little satchel of mine is enough to delight the heart of any young girl. Now, you might think that only a fancy china doll in fine clothes could do that. But you'd be wrong. Yes, ma'am, what I carry right with me is the finest line of McLoughlin paper dolls. It's a fact that all girls love paper dolls, from three or four on up. They ripen the imagination and cause the child to think and to draw and to pretend." The agent looked up at Jessee. "Now, I'm sure I don't have to tell you how children love to play pretend. My own little gran'child plays with paper dolls from morning till night and has learned to draw clothes and to color them like a real artist. Now, ma'am, you won't find a better-quality paper than our deluxe dolls is printed on. And the colors you wouldn't believe unless you was to see them for yourself." The agent stopped and cleared his throat while Jessee shifted from one foot to the other. "Do you have a little girl on the premises, ma'am?" the agent asked hopefully.

"Well . . . well, I have a girl but . . ." Jessee began and ended uncertainly.

"Don't matter what the age is, ma'am," Yule Shipton hurried on. "All girls love paper dolls."

Jessee glanced back into the front room and saw Daisy with her head close to the window, looking out at the paper doll agent. When she looked back at Yule, there was a pitiful hang-dog expression on his face.

"Ma'am, I been walking all day long and my throat is parched so's I can hardly swaller. I wonder if you could give me a little drink of water? Just a little drink of water ought to revive my physical and spiritual being right quick."

"Well. . . ," Jessee said hesitantly, frowning again.

"Then I'll be on my way, just as quick as that," Yule said when he noticed Jessee's hesitation.

"Well, all right," Jessee said finally and she pushed the screen door open for the man to enter the house. Then, turning to Daisy, who was still at the window, she said, "Go in the kitchen and get this here gent a cup of water, Daisy."

"Just call me plain 'Yule,' ma'am. I was born at

Christmas and named for the season. I don't stand on no ceremony," Yule said as he took off his hat and sat it on a nearby table. He had a full head of dark hair with not a speckle of gray in it. Jessee stared at his hair, wondering how he could appear so old and yet have none of the looks of old age.

Daisy moved quickly to do what she was told and was soon back, shyly offering Yule a cup of water. He took the cup, smiled at Daisy, and said, "Thank you, child."

Yule drank down the cool water with his eyes focused on Daisy.

When he had finished, he handed the cup back to her, saying, "Well, now. It's just amazing what a cup of the Lord's own pure water will do to revive the spirits of a man." Then he looked right into Daisy's eyes and asked, "Do you have any paper dolls, child?"

"She don't talk," Jessee said quickly, fidgeting with embarrassment.

Yule studied the deep, forlorn loneliness in Daisy's eyes for a long moment. Then he said brightly, looking at Jessee, "Don't matter. A child needn't have a speaking voice to enjoy the pleasures of paper dolls. All she has to have is eyes to see and an imagination to take her hither and yon." He gripped his suitcase. He had walked a long way and made no sales. The handle of the suitcase was slick and sweaty against his fingers. "It sure would make my day a happy one if you would allow me a minute to show these fine paper dolls to this here child."

Daisy, still holding the cup, felt her heart thump.

She shot a quick, eager glance at Jessee, who was frowning again. "I don't think so," she said and Daisy felt her heart tighten with disappointment.

Yule, looking once again into the depths of loneliness in Daisy's eyes, said, "You could never give this child ner any other a better gift than a McLoughlin paper doll, ma'am. If it's the cost that's troubling you, I can put your mind at ease. An envelope of delightful, lifelike dolls is only fifteen cents. That ain't a lot to pay for all the joy you could bring this child."

Jessee looked up and met Daisy's eyes and saw the desolation and pleading. She felt it as though it were a hunger that shouted at her from deep in the pit of her own stomach. Pangs of guilt and sadness flooded through her. If only she could be better to the girl. If only . . .

Jessee looked back at Yule. "Well, I reckon Daisy ain't got much to occupy herself with. But . . ."

"Ain't no better way for a child to take up time than to play with paper dolls, ma'am," Yule said quickly.

Jessee stared at the suitcase and began to chew on the inside of her mouth. If only Daisy were bright and pert and would talk up and say cute things and could draw and paint and go to school and sing and laugh like other girls! If only she *looked* like a normal girl! she thought painfully, as she had a hundred thousand times before.

Yule, watching Jessee's face and observing her hesitation, began to talk eagerly, adding names of the paper dolls and the style of clothing that came with them, and ended with "Just let me show them to you, ma'am. You won't be disappointed. I can guarantee it."

Jessee sighed and gave Daisy a quick glance. "Well, Daisy ain't like other girls. . . ," she tried to explain, but she could not go on.

"A little tomboy!" Yule said with a chuckle. "Why, there ain't no better way to teach a young girl the way to be a little lady than to have her play dress-up with paper dolls. Your girl will learn all the secrets of fashion in no time at all."

Fashion won't help Daisy, Jessee thought miserably. She won't never be anything but Daisy. Daisy with stringy hair. Daisy with little darting cat eyes. Daisy never saying a word. Daisy always running away. Finally she sighed and said, "Well, I reckon it won't hurt none to just look at them."

Daisy felt her heart thump again, as though it had been stopped still for a long time and had just begun to pump once more. She began to tremble with expectation. Yule smiled and said, "Now, if I can just set down on that fine-looking davenport . . ." He lifted the suitcase and laid it beside him as Jessee and Daisy moved in close. They watched with eager curiosity as he opened the suitcase and took out several long, wide envelopes. "If I could trouble you for that chair over yonder?" he said to Jessee, who went across the room and brought the tall, high-backed chair to the davenport. Yule scooted it in front of him and laid the envelopes out on it. Then he looked up at

Daisy. She was busily reading the writing on the envelopes, her eyes moving carefully from word to word, in the same way she had read all the words in Granny Henry's books of poetry.

"For the Parlor Amusement of Little Girls . . ." Daisy's eyes repeated to her brain over and over and her eyes suddenly exploded with excitement as they ran across the picture of the young girl below the writing. She was all dressed in a frilly frock with black shoes and lacy pantaloons, and there were red bows in her hair and long ringlets falling over her shoulder. Daisy had never seen anyone so beautiful. There was even a wide, friendly smile on the girl's face.

"Sit down, Daisy," Yule said. "Let me show you these wonderful little paper people. But don't mistake them words 'paper people,' child. For, once upon a time, they might of been as real as you and me." Daisy looked up and Yule was looking directly into her eyes. "Now, there really was a 'once upon a time,' for them that don't know it. It was long, long ago, beyond all time, so far away that no age could be put on it. Now, when you get accustomed to playing with these little people, they'll appear as alive to you as your own mama standing right here. They'll be your friends and confidants in no time at all."

Daisy sat cautiously on the edge of the davenport and watched intently as Yule picked up an envelope and pulled out a sheet of paper with a doll and several colorful outfits of clothes on it and showed it to her. Her eyes fled over the beautiful long green coat trimmed in white fur with a large fur muff, the peach-colored gown of shimmering silk, the red bonnet set with tall, colorful plumes and matching red cape. She became breathless and excited just looking at these things.

"My. . . ," Jessee breathed, leaning down and looking closely at the doll and clothes on the paper.

"This here is Grace," Yule said. "Look at them long curls and that fancy dress and them lacy bloomers. You'd never find the like of this little gal in drab surroundings. No sir, not this little lady."

"She is old-timey," Jessee said.

"Yes, ma'am," Yule said as he pulled a sheet of paper out of another envelope. The second envelope held a handsome boy doll and three sets of clothes, all in bright colors. "This here is Terence. Now, ain't he a good-looking lad?" He looked up at Daisy, who was staring at the paper dolls with such obvious delight that her eyes seemed to have doubled in size. "Any girl would like to have this young feller for a friend," Yule added.

Daisy's eyes ran up and down the boy paper doll. He was wearing strange, beautiful-looking clothes, just as Grace was, a pair of purple pants and a shirt with ruffles all the way down the front and at the wrists and shoes with heels and bright-looking buckles on them. If Granny Henry had seen him she would have called him "out of the ages" or "like that Shakespeare feller," Daisy thought. Granny Henry had a book of Shakespeare plays, but she could never read the words so that they made any sense and Daisy didn't like the plays as well as she liked the books of simple poems.

"Well, he's a sight, all right," Jessee said. "Just look at all them fancy clothes! Even a cape to go with them britches!"

"It depicts the finest velvet," Yule said. "Don't it look like as if you could touch it and it would be soft to your skin?" He smiled at Daisy. "Go ahead on, child, touch the cape. It looks so real."

With fearful hesitation and an unbearable desire, Daisy reached out and touched the beautiful maroon-colored cape on the paper with her finger. Her finger shook against the velvet and seemed to sink into all its softness. The paper doll agent was right. It *did* feel real! So real that a feeling of fear and awe ran all through Daisy.

Yule chuckled. "Terence here would be glad to know you took a liking to his finery. Wouldn't you, Terence?"

Daisy quickly jerked her finger away from the cape. She could have sworn the paper doll's mouth had moved and he had spoken to her!

Chapter
Eleven

"Ma'am, just look at the expression on your girl's face," Yule said to Jessee. "She'd ruther have these paper dolls than anything you could ever give her."

Jessee stared at Daisy's face. The girl looked the same to her. Jessee frowned and rubbed the back of her hand. Yule waited for her to make some comment, but she merely looked from Daisy back to the paper dolls.

"May I remind you, ma'am, that these two paper dolls is only fifteen cents each? That's only thirty cents to bring joy into your girl's life," Yule went on.

Jessee sighed. She was sure Delbert would disapprove, but . . . "Well, I reckon I can buy the girl doll."

Daisy began nodding her head fiercely and reached

out to grab up the paper holding Terence that she had just put down. She stared down into his handsome, gently smiling face. Could it be that he was saying her name, saying, "Hello, Daisy?"

"Your girl likes Terence," Yule said. "And a fine choice he is too. But I'm afraid Terence would be mighty lonesome without his friend Grace. They've been together for so long, you see."

"Oh, all right," Jessee said with the sharp sound of disgust in her voice. "I'll get the thirty cents." She hurried from the front room into her bedroom and took the change out of a coin purse in her dresser drawer.

Yule looked at Daisy. "Take good care of your new friends, Daisy. Keep them in a handy, dry place, and they'll always be there, eager and waiting to play with you. Friends for life, that's what they'll be." He began putting the other envelopes into his suitcase, aware that Daisy was still staring into Terence's face.

Friends for life . . . friends for life. . . , Daisy said over and over in her mind. No one has ever smiled at me the way you are doing, she thought as she studied Terence's smile, afraid that any moment it would suddenly break into an angry, disagreeable frown, just like the faces of real people did when they looked at her. With the tip of her finger, she touched the dark coiled curls of his hair, touched the cheeks that rose attractively with his smile, touched the chin and the indentation in it, touched the thick-looking dark eyebrows, and studied the dark eyes. Everything looked so real and felt so real. Daisy could hardly believe that Terence was made out of paper.

"I can see you've already taken a fond liking to Terence," Yule said, looking at Daisy with a wide grin. "Don't forget about Grace. She wants to be your friend too."

Daisy reached for the paper with Grace and her clothes on it and held it close to study the girl. Grace's smile was as bright and friendly as Terence's was and her eyes crinkled at the corners, giving her a merry look. In fact, Daisy thought, Grace looked very much like Granny Henry looked in those old pictures that had been taken of her when she was young. She wished she had a picture of Granny Henry now.

Jessee came back into the front room with the change and handed it to Yule. He pulled a pad and pencil out of his jacket pocket, set it on the chair seat, and leaned over to write on it, all the while praising the quality of the paper dolls. When he had finished making out the bill of sale, he tore the page out of the pad and handed it to Jessee.

"Looky there, ma'am," he said as he put the pad and pencil back into his pocket. "Your girl is friends with Terence and Grace already."

Jessee could see that Daisy was totally absorbed in the paper dolls. It was as if she were all alone with the two dolls and as if there were some silent communication going on between them.

Yule stood up to go and said, "You won't never be sorry you bought them paper dolls for that child, ma'am. Never a moment of the day or night will you bemoan having spent that thirty cents." He reached for Jessee's hand and pumped it heartily.

Then he pulled his hat off the table and set it on his head.

All at once Daisy erupted into flight, bursting across the room and out the door. Yule laughed. "See there? Whipped right out of here to play with them paper dolls already!"

Jessee frowned and tried to see Daisy through the screen door, but she had already disappeared from the yard. Maybe she hadn't done the right thing, Jessee thought. Paper dolls wouldn't do a girl that was about to be married any good.

"Much obliged, ma'am. Good to do business with you. I'll be back around in these parts in another six months to a year. I reckon by then that girl of yourn will be ready to add to her collection," Yule said, tipping his hat to Jessee. Then he stepped out the door and went down the steps of the porch and across the yard, swinging his satchel at his side.

Jessee watched him from the doorway, shaking her head. "That feller sure is a strange one," she thought.

Chapter
Twelve

As Elmer walked along, high-stepping it up the hill road, whistling and feeling as though he could lick the world and everyone in it, he could see the huge old mansion getting closer. It was only late afternoon and the sun was still up, but an eerie darkness seemed to cover the whole place as though a cloak had been thrown over it to keep the sunlight away. Lights in the lower floor of the mansion peeped through the heavy tangles of vines and trees that shrouded everything.

The Howard mansion had been around since the turn of the century and, year after year, had fallen into such decay that all the upper rooms had to be closed off out of fear they would suddenly collapse and go tumbling down over the lower part of the house. The property had belonged to the Howard girls' great-grandfather, who had been a vintner and raised the richest and finest grapes in the valley. While he was alive, he gave parties and picnics and invited the whole county to take part in the grape-harvesting festivities. After his death, his only child and son, the grandfather of the Howard girls, showed no interest in planting and harvesting grapes and spent his entire life traveling and spending the fortune his father had worked for. After the death of his son's wife, the elder Howard led his grandson, Bartholomew, down the path of least resistance, never requiring that he work or advance in any way in life. When he, Bartholomew, grew up, he married a woman of high class from New Orleans, set her up in the mansion, and there she bore him three daughters. When she died, long before she was middle-aged, the three daughters were already well on their way to being just like their father and their grandfather, spoiled, idle, and lazy. They were educated in a convent, were ignorant of life, and were selfish and demanding. They were also jealous of their father's attention. By the time they were grown, the family money had all but been squandered away and the mansion was in ruin.

The verdant land now lay hard-clotted and covered with wreaths of weeds and row upon row of rotted stumps of what once produced the fat, succulent grapes. The whole place had withered into a decaying sadness that matched that of the Howard girls. Although only in their early forties, they were homely, bedraggled-looking old maids, living as though they were young, rich, and beautiful and sought after by handsome young men. They dressed daily as if a suitor were coming to call, as though a party were being given, and as though their lives were moving at a fast, exciting pace. But in reality, their existence was dreary. As dreary as the rooms of the old mansion.

Only rarely did a young man straggle up the hill to the mansion and meet the Howard sisters. Once there, he became puzzled and a little frightened by their excitable manner and their obvious competition with one another, and disgusted and annoyed that they were not really "girls" at all but sallow old women who twittered and carried on like immature children.

Because the Howard sisters never went into town and because people in Vineyard Flats were rarely, if ever, invited to the mansion, people maintained their belief that, somehow, the Howard girls were still young and the family was still wealthy. They often saw old man Howard, "Bart," as he was called, standing in the dust at the small depot waiting for a train to take him off somewhere. He seemed not to have changed over the years. Time seemed not to pass for the Howards as it did for everyone else.

Elmer approached the veranda of the old mansion with a slack grin on his face and went up the steps shoving long, drooping wisteria vines out of his way. The vines looped in and out of the tall columns that supported the roof and emitted a sad fragrance over everything. Elmer sniffed several times as he went up to the door and raised the large tarnished knocker and pounded it against the old wood three loud, insistent times. He snickered to himself when he thought of how before today he had never had the nerve to even step a foot on the long road that led up the hill. Before today he had felt too poor. But with just one sip from the brandy bottle, he now felt as rich as anyone. He had heard a few whispered stories that certain men told about meeting the Howard sisters and finding them old and ugly, but he had scoffed at them and refused to believe such tales. After all, the Howards were the Howards.

He raised the knocker again and gave it another loud crack against the door. His mother would be right proud, he thought, that he had finally gotten the gumption to pay a visit.

The door came open on the last knock and Elmer stared into the face of Irma Howard with a start. The grin on his face was replaced by a look of surprise and shock. Irma Howard's hair was graying close to her face and was pulled up into a tight knot on the top of her head. The knot, Elmer observed critically, looked like someone had dumped a small pile of salt and pepper into it. Below the woman's eyes and around her mouth, he could see tiny spidery lines of age. Maybe he was mistaken, he thought hopefully. Maybe this was a maid or the Howards' cook. But before he could ask, another face popped around the door.

"Oh!" Irene Howard said with delight. "We have a caller!" Her smile gave her long, narrow face a more pleasant look. She appeared older than Irma, Elmer thought, and much thinner. Her hair was all of one shade, short and curly. But her eyes were the same dull, grayish color as her sister's.

Elmer was pretty sure now that the two were sisters and not a cook or maid. They looked too much alike not to be related. He moved from foot to foot, feeling disappointment that what he had heard in town was indeed true. The sisters *were* old.

Suddenly another face appeared from around the door and Elmer could see that this was the oldest-looking sister of all. A sagging double chin drooped loosely at her throat and her hair was gray and puffed all around her face like a frizzy bouquet. Her eyes were the eyes of a woman who did close work, Elmer thought, like tatting and embroidery. They were a little bloodshot, but were the same uninteresting gray as her two sisters' eyes were. By now there was no mistaking it. This woman had to be the third Howard "girl." No wonder there were nasty jokes about them! Elmer suddenly remembered what his mother had repeated to him so often. "Them girls will be left a handy sum of money when old man Howard dies." Remembering that, Elmer grinned broadly.

"Well, isn't someone going to invite this young man in?" Ivy Howard asked, raising her head and looking down her nose at her sisters.

"Oh, do come in!" Irene said, giving Ivy a slight shove out of the way so that she could stand in the center of the doorway.

Irma moved closer and gave Irene a push that sent her backward into Ivy and said, "Please step inside, Mister . . . Mister?"

Elmer chuckled and wiped his nose on his shirt-sleeve. "I'm Elmer Goots from out south of town," he said, proudly throwing his shoulders back and entering the door.

The three sisters stepped back, allowing Elmer to enter the vestibule and, observing Elmer's short pants and tousled red hair more closely, they twittered and giggled among themselves as they led him into the parlor. But Elmer did not notice. He was too filled with awe at having been invited into the old mansion.

The sisters made a big production of seating Elmer in a comfortable chair and serving him tea in an elegant cup and saucer. They sat down side by side across from him on a floral covered divan with their hands folded primly in their laps, watching with eager eyes and smiles of anticipation while he glanced around the large room. The room was filled with old, ornate furniture, lacy antimacassars on the chairs and divan, tables that dripped with embroidered scarves, lamps with faded shades, and heavy draperies that hung loosely from the windows, their once bright pattern now almost erased by age. Elmer's eyes skirted over the wallpaper that was torn in places and held ghostly pale spots where once photographs had hung. Everything seemed to belong to another time, Elmer thought. A time he had never been a part of. He had never seen any room like this one, where everything was both beautiful and ugly at the same time. But the fact of the matter was, he had never seen any room any time in his life like this one. Nor had he ever seen women quite like the Howard sisters.

"Sisters and I are so happy to meet you, Elmer," Irma said, and Elmer's glance was drawn back to the three women perched on the divan across from him.

"I can speak for myself!" Irene said testily while giving Irma a narrow, down-her-nose look.

"I am the oldest and I should speak first!" Ivy said in an angry tone. And, pulling her spiteful eyes away from her sisters and raising them to Elmer, she asked, "What business are you in, Elmer?"

"Well . . . er . . . ah . . . I ain't in no business," Elmer answered, feeling the bottle of brandy poking him uncomfortably in his ribs.

"Then what do you do?" Ivy went on.

"You asked the last question!" Irene snapped, giving Ivy a scowl. "Let me ask that!" She turned back to Elmer with a smile. "What do you do, Elmer?" Her voice was sweet and pleasant.

"Oh, I work around ranches and such as that. Break in horses and so on," Elmer lied breezily. The teacup that he had balanced on his knee felt hot and the bottle under his shirt hard, and he felt like another drink.

"My, that is interesting," Irma said, turning to give her sisters a disappointed look. All their lives the sisters had waited for a charming young man to come into their lives who was well educated, well traveled, and wealthy. But now, in declining age, they were willing to accept any manner of man. Even young Elmer Goots!

"But dangerous," Irene said matter-of-factly.

"Don't you think Elmer *knows* that?" Ivy asked disgustedly.

"Aw, shoot! It ain't that bad," Elmer said and chuckled.

"How *brave* you must be to break in wild horses!" all three "girls" echoed at the same time.

Elmer chuckled again. These old Howard girls sure were something, he thought as he studied each one. They were as homely as any old woman he'd ever seen on the streets of Vineyard Flats, and all three setting there as proper as the ladies in church on a Sunday morning. And looking at him like they believed every word he was telling them. Shoot, he snickered to himself, he hadn't ever even looked a wild horse in the face, much less tried to tame one.

"Would you girls like a little snort out of this bottle of brandy I brought?" Elmer asked abruptly and the girls began to titter and make little remarks behind their hands to each other. Elmer set the cup of tea on a table beside his chair and leaned back slightly to pull the bottle out from under his shirt. "They is plenty here for everyone," he said, holding the bottle up for them to see.

"Get the wine goblets," Ivy directed her sisters and Irene snapped, "*You* get the goblets!"

"Yes!" Irma said. "You never do anything but sit and talk and try to keep the attention of every gentleman who comes to call!"

"That is a *lie,* sister!" Ivy exploded with her face red and her back suddenly as stiff as a ramrod.

"It is *not* a lie, Ivy Howard!" Irene accused. "You think while we are getting the goblets you'll be priming Elmer for yourself!"

Ivy jumped up from the divan and shook her round, knotted fist in Irene's face. "Don't you say that, you mean beast!"

"Don't you hit me! I'll tell Father!" Irene cried, drawing back.

"Leave sister be!" Irma shouted.

"You're both jealous! Just jealous! You've always been jealous of me, thinking I'd get married first!" Ivy shouted back.

"That is not true, sister!" Irene said in a shaking voice.

Elmer watched the sisters with wide-eyed amusement.

"The truth of the matter is," Irma said evenly as she reached up and adjusted her mound of salt-and-pepper hair, "you are *both* jealous of me and you always have been."

"You!" the two other sisters exploded in unison. "Jealous of an *old biddy* like you?" They began to laugh loudly and Ivy fell back onto the divan and covered her mouth with her hands, laughing uncontrollably.

Irma glared at her sisters with fury on her face. "Bah!" she cried, opening her mouth wide and throwing her eyes toward the ceiling. "Bah! And bah, again!"

Elmer chuckled rawly at the picture of the three old hens setting on the divan squabbling back and forth like little children. Finally he said, "Now, you gals just simmer down. I come to see all of y'all."

Upon hearing Elmer's voice, the three sisters

quieted and stiffened, and Ivy said with a superior thrust of her head, "We do *not* share, Elmer. You must make a decision as to which one of us you wish to court."

"Yes! Yes!" Irma and Irene agreed, nodding their heads up and down.

Elmer's mouth fell open. *Court?* He was already six feet deep into an agreement with old man Heath over that Daisy Flowerdew! Now, here he was with three old women looking to be courted by him! He'd never seen the like!

"You gals looking to get hitched?" he asked with squinted-eye caution as he surveyed each old, wrinkled face.

"Of course," Ivy answered.

"Certainly," Irma said.

"Indeed we are," Irene joined in.

Elmer snickered and turned his head from side to side. No sir, he'd never seen the like! Before he could decide what to say, the front door of the house opened and footsteps sounded in the vestibule.

"Papa!" the sisters cried out in delighted unison and they began to adjust their skirts and to pat their hair and to sit up straight.

"Girls, I'm home!" A strong, cheerful male voice floated from the vestibule and Elmer looked around, quickly shoving the bottle under his shirt.

Chapter Thirteen

"Good evening, girls," Bart Howard said as he entered the parlor with a broad smile on his old but still handsome face.

"Good evening, Papa!" the sisters sang out, their faces bright from seeing their father again. He had been away on a short trip to gamble and visit friends. Tiredness showed around his eyes, but they were still bright and snapping with all his zest for life.

Irma stood up and went to give her father a hug and a peck on his cheek.

"And who have we here?" Bart asked, seeing Elmer setting in a chair and feeling Irma's kiss at the same time.

"This is young Elmer Goots, Papa," Irma answered.

Bart went to shake Elmer's hand and Irene whis-

pered across to him, "You are supposed to stand up."
But Elmer did not stand.

"Oh, I'm fine just like I am," he said, and Irene
frowned.

"Elmer has come to court me, Papa," Ivy said to
Bart after rising to give him a warm hug.

"No, he has *not!*" Irene cried, flying up from the
divan to kiss her father. "Elmer has come to court
me, Papa!"

"Girls . . . girls!" Bart said with an indulgent
smile. He was very short and thin and stooped, and
his hair was a thin fluff of white that circled the sides
and back of his head. On top, he was totally bald. He
wore a suit that had once been white. Now it was a
faded yellow-gray. The old man stood before Elmer,
pumping his hand. "A pleasure to meet you, Mr.
Goots," he said in a friendly manner.

"Papa," Ivy said, hooking her arm through her father's arm. "I must speak to you *alone.*"

Irene and Irma sniffed loudly at their sister and gave
her a menacing glare.

"Of course, my child," Bart said and to Elmer he
said, "Excuse us, please. My daughter seems impatient." He bowed slightly, and Elmer chuckled at his
formality.

Irene and Irma sat down on the divan, exchanged a
suspicious look, then turned to stare after their father
and sister. A moment later, when they were out of
the room, Ivy could be heard telling her father in a
loud, agitated voice, "Elmer has come to court *me,*
Papa. Irma and Irene won't let us alone. How am I

ever going to get a husband with such jealous sisters?"

"Listen to that old snit!" Irma said angrily, turning to Irene. "Saying such things to Papa! Even *he* knows she couldn't get a man before either of us could!"

"The brazen old hussy! She never could keep her voice down or even keep a secret," Irene said nastily. "*She's* the jealous one!"

"I'm older than the two of them. It's only fair and right that I be courted *before* them!" Ivy went on in her nervous, loud voice.

"Dear child, there is no reason to raise the quills on your sweet little neck. You three girls leave me alone with that young man and I'll find out just what his motives are." Bart's voice rang out gently from the vestibule. He spoke with the strength of a man who had confronted the same situation many times.

"Oh, all right, Papa," Ivy said grudgingly.

When they returned to the parlor Bart said, "Now, run along to bed and let your old Papa have a little nip out of that bottle Mr. Goots has under his shirt. I'll speak to each one of you tomorrow."

Ivy left the room first, firmly believing that Elmer had come to court her and her alone. Irma and Irene went slowly, as though they were being sent against their will, whispering to each other in scathing tones.

After they had gone Elmer pulled the bottle of brandy from under his shirt, offered it to Bart, and said, "You sent them daughters of yourn to bed just like as if they was little biddy young'uns."

"In a way they are," Bart said, accepting the bottle.

He wiped the mouth of it off with a faded handkerchief that he pulled out of his jacket pocket and took a long drink of the brandy. When he brought the bottle down from his mouth, he said, "Elmer, my boy, let us go out onto the veranda, where our voices will not be echoed through this old house and heard by the girls."

Elmer got up out of his chair and followed Bart out of the house to the veranda. They sat in white wicker chairs with low, sunken seats. Loose wicker stuck Elmer sharply in his back. He edged around until he found a spot where the wicker lay flat and sank into the chair. It was getting dark and the fragrance of the wisteria fell over the porch, sagging on the long vines. Near the steps crickets talked incessantly to each and a little breeze brushing through the tall oak trees made a melancholy swish . . . swish . . . swish sound. Elmer felt pleasantly relaxed, listening to Bart Howard speak.

"I know you haven't come up here to court a one of my daughters, Elmer Goots. A boy your age couldn't possibly be interested in my girls. I'm not the foolish old man you may think I am—a person would have to get up pretty early in the day to put one over on me. Harsh as it may sound, it is my girls who are the foolish ones. It saddens me to say it, Elmer, but I gave up the hope long ago that they would find husbands. There isn't a suitable man in nine counties who'd even care to court them."

Bart stopped and sighed deeply. "I indulge my girls, Elmer, let them have company and little parties, and provide them with folderol to keep them content. They'll outlive me, certainly, and be left alone here in this old ramshackle mausoleum until they pass on. But, I tell you, Elmer, not one of them will be taken advantage of!" Bart's voice rose suddenly and his chin shot up as he spoke. "I've provided only for their basic needs, a little trip now and then, a new dress, a few trinkets, but not a penny more. My wishes will go into effect, through my will, the very day I am carried down from this hill in a box. Do you hear what I am saying, Elmer?"

"Yes, sir. You bet your boots I hear what you're saying," Elmer answered, nodding his head up and down.

"Good," Bart said and leaned back in his wicker chair and went on in a calmer voice. "That will of mine will discourage any man who thinks he can come up here and hoodwink my daughters. There have been troops of fellers young and old, up and down this hill over the years, thinking they could get their hands on my money. After our little talks, most of them never came back. Those that did merely came for the food and drinks they could get. It's not that way much anymore, Elmer. You are the first young feller who's been up here in some time." Bart leaned forward, looking intently into Elmer's face. "Now, young man, why *did* you come up here?"

"Well, sir, my ma always wanted me to," Elmer admitted, feeling his tongue loosen enough to be honest. "I reckon Ma thought your daughters was younger than they is. Ain't too many folks ever seen them and, living out south of town, Ma don't get all the gossip. Ain't nobody I know of ever seen them on the streets in town. I heard some fellers talk once in a while, but you can't trust certain fellers to tell the truth, not even if you was to try to knock it into their heads."

"My sentiments exactly, Elmer," Bart said, crossing his legs and swinging one foot. "You came up here because your mama wanted you to, eh?"

"Yes, sir, I did."

"You don't have a wife or a girlfriend?"

Elmer thought guiltily of Delbert Heath and that Daisy Flowerdew he was expected to marry. "Well. . . ," he said hesitantly. "They is this man who wants me to hitch up with his stepdaughter, but . . ." Elmer stopped and scratched his head.

"But what, my boy?"

"I ain't het up on it," Elmer answered, careful not to mention the ten-dollar deal with Delbert and the fact that he hadn't even met Daisy.

Bart took another swallow out of the bottle. "Marriage is a good proposition. Keeps a man on the straight and narrow. What holds you back?"

"Well, a feller likes to get out in life and live a little, do a few things first, I reckon." Elmer's mind swung back to the ten-dollar deal again. "Oh, I reckon it'll take place. Don't see how it won't with her folks wanting it so bad." He sighed deeply, thinking, there's more truth than poetry in that.

Bart leaned forward and said eagerly, "When it's all arranged, let me know where the wedding reception will be held. I haven't been to a wedding party in years."

"Well . . . er . . . huh?" Elmer asked, looking puzzled.

"The reception, the festivities. Where are they going to be held?"

"Ain't going to be none that I know of," Elmer answered.

"No party? No fun? We can't have that, my boy. Let me have the pleasure of offering my home to your wedding party."

"Well . . . I dunno . . ."

"We'll have a fine party. My girls are wonderful cooks. We'll prepare everything. How does that sound to you, Elmer?"

Elmer gulped. He didn't want any party and he didn't want to marry that Daisy Flowerdew. Without waiting for his answer, Bart went on. "There is nothing so fine as a spring wedding. My own wedding to my girls' mother was in the spring. April. We had a grand ball. Everyone danced the night away. . . ."

As Bart rambled on, Elmer suddenly remembered that he was supposed to go back to Dogtown Road the next day and meet Daisy. He didn't want any wedding party and he didn't want to meet that Daisy!

"When you get things arranged, let me know. I'll tell my girls to prepare for short notice. Bring as many people as you like. The more the merrier. And don't worry about my girls. The festivities will soon put a cap on their desires." Bart continued and Elmer, suddenly yawning, leaned his head against the chair and listened to the crickets and the sound of the wind in the trees. Bart Howard sure knew how to talk. The evening grew late. And after a time, the two lapsed into sleep, rolling their heads to the side and snoring loudly.

In their bedroom, the Howard sisters talked into the darkness for a long time. "Don't worry, girls, things will be fine for me after Papa's talk with Elmer," Ivy said abruptly, just as they were all beginning to doze off. She slept on a small bed while her sisters slept on a larger one.

Suddenly a pillow went flying through the air, hitting Ivy in her face. "Fool!" Irma cried into the darkness. "Elmer Goots wants me!"

Irene sat up in bed and pounded her fists into the quilt. "You are both fools! It is plain to see, Elmer wants me!"

All at once the pillow came flying back across the room, landing on Irene's head. She screamed wildly and pounded her fists harder into the quilt while Irma grabbed the pillow and shoved it angrily beneath her head. In a little while the room was still except for the uninterrupted snoring of the three sisters.

Soon dawn moved across the flatlands and climbed the hill. When Elmer opened his eyes, he found a wisteria petal dripping in his face, tickling his nose. He swept it aside and stood up. Everything was bright with daylight. He glanced down at Bart, slumped in his chair, snoring above the rooster that crowed in the distance. It would be a long walk home in the hot sun. He walked to the edge of the porch and went stumbling down the steps, across the yard, and down the road that led away from the old mansion.

"Soon as I get home, I'm going to flop myself in bed and I ain't going to crawl out till after a month of Sundays has passed," Elmer said to himself as he shoved his hands into his pockets and began to walk a little faster. "No sir," he went on as he watched his new boots tap into the dusty road, "Ma's own good-smelling beans and cornbread won't even be able to pull me out of bed. I'm going to sleep the whole day away."

And that is exactly what he did.

Chapter
Fourteen

The next day, Delbert couldn't wait to get the store closed and get home to find out if Elmer had been back out to the house to meet Daisy. Elmer had beat him out of the clothes and boots and that ten dollars he had so foolishly given him. "You be back out to my place right tomorrow," he had warned Elmer when he left the store with all those new clothes. He never had told Jessee about the clothes, just that Elmer would be back, all right. He had been short and cranky with the customers for the last half of the day, so nervous was he to get home and find out everything from Jessee.

When he pulled the car into the front yard, he saw Daisy jump up from the steps of the porch and run around the house out of sight. He was glad to have her run off like that, he thought. He could talk to

Jessee easier with her not around. He got out of the car and went up to the house. He found Jessee setting beside the radio listening intently as he entered the front room.

"Turn that thing off!" Delbert shouted. The music was so loud he could hardly hear his own voice above it.

Jessee looked up, noticing Delbert for the first time, and turned the radio off. "Oh, honeybee, I didn't know you was here!" Jessee said in surprise. She got up and gave Delbert a kiss on his cheek.

"I got to talk to you," Delbert snapped and he went into the kitchen and poured himself a cup of coffee.

Jessee followed. "That song was almost over, honeybee. You know how much I love Hank Williams," she said and pouted.

"Forget about Hank Williams!" Delbert growled. "Was that Elmer Goots out here today?"

"No, he weren't, honey bear," Jessee answered, seeing the anger on Delbert's face.

"You mean, he didn't even show up?" Delbert's voice rose. He turned away from the stove with his cup of coffee and slumped down at the table.

"Why, no, I ain't seen Elmer since yesterday when he first come out here to see Daisy. I waited all day because you said he'd come back. But he didn't."

Delbert jumped up. "I knowed it! I had a feeling I was being duped by that low-down mangy dog!"

"What did he do, honey bear? Sit down. Don't get so excited. Tell me what he did," Jessee pleaded.

Delbert sank down into the chair again and stared into the dark brown coffee in his cup. "Well, I didn't tell you right away, but I allowed that no-account Elmer to put one over on me. He said he'd come back to meet Daisy for sure if I'd let him break in them boots I've had in the store for a year or more." He look up, adding guiltily, "I even give him a shirt and pants to wear and that damned ten dollars he weaseled out of me!"

"You paid him already?" Jessee asked in surprise.

"He pity-talked me out of it, the little devil!"

"Does that mean he ain't going to marry Daisy?" Jessee asked with frowns of worry creasing her face.

Delbert looked up. "It means, if he don't, I'll beat nine kinds of hell out of his low-down hide!" he said, grinding the words savagely around his tongue. He got up and went into the bedroom and came out with his long black whip in his hand. It had been his father's whip and he had kept it for years hanging on the wall.

"Delbert!" Jessee cried, glaring at the whip that sprang back and forth at Delbert's side as he stormed out of the kitchen and out of the house, working the muscles in his jaws and narrowing his eyes over everything. Jessee ran after him, crying out to him, but he ignored her and got into the car and drove away, raising up dirt like a torrent of smoke behind him.

"Oh, honey bear, come back! Come back!" Jessee cried into the swirling dust as she ran to the fence and watched the dust trailing the car until it settled and the car was out of sight.

A little while later, Olive Goots was sweeping her front-room floor when she heard a knock at the door. She set her broom against the wall and went to open it.

"Where's that ornery, no-good, red-headed son of yourn?" Delbert demanded before Olive could even open her mouth in greeting.

"Why, what on earth has come over you to yell at me like this, Delbert?" Olive cried.

Without answering, Delbert reached out and jerked the screen door open, shoved past Olive, and stomped into Elmer's bedroom, swinging the whip at his side. There he is, he thought, as he stared down at the tousled red hair and the freckled face that lay sticking out just above the quilt. There's that no-good lying little sneak!

"Wake up!" Delbert shouted and he cracked the whip at his side so hard that it seemed to snap the air in two.

From the doorway Olive cried out, "Lord of mercy! What's come over you, Delbert?"

"This here lazy whelp had better get his hind end out of bed or I'll whup him out!" Delbert threatened in answer.

Elmer had wakened the first moment he had heard footsteps in his room, but he lay still, trying not even to breathe. Now he cautiously opened one eye and stared into Delbert's red, menacing face. Should I get up or keep on playing possum, he wondered, trembling in terror.

"You leave my son be, you crazy man!" Olive

cried, rushing at Delbert and grabbing his arm and pulling on it. But Delbert jerked his arm out of Olive's grasp.

"If that slimy little thieving snake in the grass ain't out of that bed on the count of *three,* I'll put him through the mattress in pieces with one swipe!" Delbert blasted and he cracked the whip again. This time it seemed to cut right through Elmer's brain.

Olive jumped to the bed and started shaking Elmer violently. "Elmer! Elmer! Get up, boy, before this crazy man kills you!" she yelled hysterically.

Elmer opened his eyes all the way and asked, "Wha . . . what's going on, Ma?" as though there had been no cracking whip and no Delbert Heath ominously standing over him.

Delbert cracked the whip again and shouted "*ONE!*" to the top of his lungs.

"Oh, my Lord! Get up!" Olive shouted, pulling and jerking furiously at Elmer.

"What's going on here?" Elmer asked, raising up a little and peering down at the whip Delbert held. Inside he was quaking and jolting around like a chicken with its head cut off, but outwardly he appeared merely surprised.

"*TWO!*" Delbert shouted and cracked the whip again.

"Get up!" Olive begged.

"*THREE!*" Delbert exploded and he cracked the whip three loud, horrible, menacing times. Suddenly Elmer was out of the bed and on his feet with Olive hanging onto him, shuddering against him. "That's better, you durned stinking little conniver!" Delbert shouted with fire spitting from his eyes.

"Wha . . . what's a-all this a-about?" Elmer croaked, staring at Delbert in terror.

"You know what it's about!" Delbert shouted, shoving his chin forward and squaring off his legs as if he was getting ready for a fight. "If you ain't over at Judge Angelo's office first thing in the morning to marry Daisy Flowerdew, I'll string you up in the middle of town so's everyone can see what a thieving little coward you are! You hear me?" Delbert's chin came even closer to Elmer's face.

"I . . . er . . . I h-hear you," Elmer stuttered. He was shaking so hard now that his teeth were clicking in his head. He clung to Olive as tightly as she was clinging to him.

"Did you buy that Daisy gal a ring the way you was aiming to?" Delbert demanded.

"Well . . . er . . ."

"And did you buy her posies and candy?"

"Well . . . I . . ."

"Boy, you have placed your life in jeopardy!" Delbert said in a low, even voice and his nose came so close to Elmer's that Elmer could smell the sweat on the tip of it.

Delbert's words were like a gong in Elmer's ears. Beside him, Olive began to weep and moan.

Delbert moved away from Elmer and tapped the whip against his thigh. "When you show up tomorrow, you be sure you have them boots and them clothes you wheedled out of me!" he said.

"Y-you m-mean, I can't *keep* them c-clothes?" Disappointment shot through Elmer's fear-strained face.

"Boy, the only thing you're going to keep is care of Daisy Flowerdew from now on!" Delbert answered and he turned to walk to the door. At the door he turned around and, tapping the whip threateningly against his thigh again, said, "You remember what I told you! Be at the judge's office first thing in the morning *or else!*"

As soon as they heard the front door open and close Olive cried, "Look what you got yourself into, Elmer! You ain't even laid eyes on that Daisy Flowerdew and now you have to hitch up with her!"

Elmer moved away from Olive and sank to the edge of the bed like an empty potato sack. He could only stare in glum silence at the new shirt and pants slung across a nearby chair and at the boots that sat on the floor beside it.

Chapter Fifteen

The moment Daisy had seen Delbert's car coming down the road to the house she jumped up off the porch steps and took off running to Toby's Creek. In her hands were the two envelopes holding the paper dolls Jessee had bought for her. When she reached the creek, she hurried to set down near the thicket of desert willow bushes. She would never be found here, she thought, near the fragrant pink and lavender flowers that grew on the bushes and the shade the long, drooping leaves cast over her. The grass was damp against her overalls, but she didn't care. She was too happy to be all alone with Terence and Grace.

Slowly and carefully, she opened the envelope Terence was in and gently took him out. The night before, in her back-porch room, she had cut out both the paper dolls and sat on the bed for hours merely staring into their beautiful faces. Their smiles, directed only at her, did not change or waver into angry scowls or rejecting sneers, not in all the time she sat looking at them. Now she knew what it was like to have friends and to have them smile at her and not call her names or move disgustedly away from her. Last night she did not speak a word to them, did not dress them in their beautiful clothes, so content and filled with the magic of their smiles was she. But now she wanted to talk to them, to tell them how she loved them and how happy she was to have them for her friends.

She held Terence in the palm of her hand and looked straight into his eyes. "Hello, Terence," she said softly, smiling back at his smile.

"I thought you'd never speak to me, Daisy!" Terence said and Daisy's eyes popped wide. "I kept hoping you would last night when you kept looking at us, but you didn't. We have to be spoken to before we can speak to you. Now won't you please let Grace out of that awful envelope she's mashed into?"

"Oh, yes!" Daisy said at once, looking uncertain and wondering if she were really hearing the voice of the paper doll. He had a funny, old-fashioned way of speaking.

"Just put me down in the grass, Daisy. I'll be all right. It's nice here. Very pleasant."

Daisy very carefully set Terence on the grass and leaned him against a leaf of the desert willow bush. Then she opened the other envelope to take Grace out. When the paper doll was out of the envelope and in Daisy's palm, Grace said, "At last! It is no fun being covered back and front by that stiff paper. Hello, Daisy. I'm glad to meet you. Will you put my lovely blue satin dress on me today? Please? I'm so tired of wearing the same thing."

"Grace likes to change clothes five times a day and more," Terence said and laughed, looking up from the grass at Daisy.

"I . . . I'll have to wait until I go back to the house, where the scissors are," Daisy said, wondering if this would offend Grace.

"She *can* speak, Terence! She truly can," Grace said with a delighted look of surprise on her pretty face. "Don't forget now, I want to wear the blue dress first."

"Oh, I won't forget, Grace," Daisy promised.

"Bring Grace down here, Daisy. Let us stand beside this giant of a tree," Terence said.

Daisy had to smile. The "tree" was really the desert willow bush. But she did as she was asked, standing Grace up in the grass and leaning her against the long leaves of the bush.

"I've never seen anyone stare at us the way you do, Daisy," Terence said.

"Yes. Why do you stare at us so, Daisy?" Grace asked.

"I . . . well, I ain't had no friends before. And . . ."

"No friends?" Terence asked and Daisy saw him look at Grace. At the same time, Grace turned to look at him. Then they looked back up at Daisy.

"Well . . . what I mean is, I had Granny Henry for

a friend, but she passed on. She was all I had," Daisy tried to explain.

"But you have a mother and a father," Grace said. "I saw them."

"Delbert ain't my real daddy. Granny Henry said my real daddy was a aimless and reckless man. The woman, Jessee, is my mama, but she don't like to be. She wants to be all alone with Delbert. She wants to marry me off so's she won't have to put up with me." Tears sprang into Daisy's eyes and she sniffled hard, trying to force them back.

"Don't cry, Daisy!" Grace said and her small face seemed to crumple.

"This is monstrous!" Terence cried, indignantly using a word Daisy had seen in one of Granny Henry's books. "When do you have to marry?"

"I don't know. Anytime now. I ain't been told yet," Daisy answered, wiping the tears away.

"How can we help you, Daisy?" Terence asked, looking at Daisy as though he were feeling the exact pain that she felt.

"Ain't no one can help me," Daisy said miserably.

"There is always a way, Daisy. It is up to us to think of it," Terence said, looking thoughtful.

"Oh, I'm so glad you're my friends!" Daisy said in a burst of gratitude. Then she hung her head. "But I don't think they is anything anyone can do. I done been sold."

"Sold?" Terence and Grace asked in puzzled unison.

"Delbert put a sign in the store winder offering to

give anyone who would marry me ten dollars. He already took it down—for the red-headed boy. It's him I have to marry," Daisy said, raising her head.

"Oh, my!" Grace said with a frown and added a "Tsh, tsh" with her tongue.

"Daisy, don't fret. Grace and I will think of something. We won't let them do this to you," Terence said and Daisy saw the look of concern on his handsome face.

"It's too terrible to imagine!" Grace said, shaking her head, and suddenly Daisy remembered a poem she had seen in one of Granny Henry's books. It began,

> *Too terrible to imagine*
> *A heart broken in two . . .*

Oh! If only she had the book of poems that Aunt Lou had taken! Granny Henry's fingerprints and little coffee spills were all in it. Having the book, she would have something of Granny Henry. She hung her head again and tried not to cry.

"Oh, please don't cry, Daisy! If you cry, I shall cry too. And I don't want to cry!" Grace said.

"I'll try not to," Daisy said, raising her head and sighing deeply. "But it seems like nothing ever works out right. It never has. Not since Granny Henry died."

"If you could have three wishes, what would they be, Daisy?" Terence asked suddenly, his face brightened by his smile again.

"First of all, I'd wish for Granny Henry not to die.

But I know that can't be now. The next thing after that, I'd wish not to marry that red-haired boy. And, after that, I'd wish to have Granny Henry's book of poems I brought with me when I come here to live. It fell out of my box of things and Aunt Lou took it back to Punkin Center with her." Daisy sighed and frowned at the grass. "But it don't do no good to make no wishes."

"You have to believe in wishes, Daisy," Grace said softly.

"You wished for friends, didn't you?" Terence asked. "Well, here we are." He opened his arms and spread them wide.

Daisy had to smile at Terence's beautiful face and funny old-fashioned clothes and at Grace, who looked so friendly with her eyes twinkling and her curls bobbing. She was so grateful, so thankful for her new friends.

Grace started to giggle and Terence joined in with his husky laughter. Soon Daisy was brushing her tears away and laughing too. It was wonderful to laugh with her friends, she thought. Wonderful and magic.

Daisy stayed at Toby's Creek until the sun sank in the sky and she knew she had to go back to the house. "Be very careful when you put us inside those envelopes, Daisy," Terence cautioned her. But he didn't have to. Daisy knew she would protect Terence and Grace with her own life. And, if she could, she would press them to her heart and carry them with her forever.

Chapter
Sixteen

Early the next morning Jessee woke Daisy and told her, "This is a special day for you, Daisy, honey. This is the day you get married."

Daisy sat up in bed with the look of terror on her face. Married? Today? Thoughts jerked backward and forward in her brain so fast that she couldn't make any sense out of them. All she knew was that Jessee had told her she was to be married this very day.

"I've got a pretty dress for you to wear that used to be mine. And some flowers to carry and even a pair of shoes that I can't wear no more," Jessee went on with a cheery smile on her face. She was already dressed in a pretty pale green dress that flowed out from her waist and rippled around her legs when she moved. Her platinum hair was a frizz of curls that bobbed like a bouncing ball. "I was just a year older than you are when I first had thoughts about marrying your daddy, as no-account as he was."

Tell me about my daddy! Daisy wanted to shout. Tell me more than just he was aimless and reckless and wandering! But she could only shout with her eyes and Jessee could not hear what they said.

"Well, I reckon you'll be living with Miz Goots. . . ," Jessee went on, flouncing up and down the floor, the skirt of her dress swinging around her legs. "She ain't a bad woman and well . . . I got to tell you, Daisy, honey, you're mighty lucky to get a husband. Elmer looks strong and he's young. He'll make a good man for you. Now, I want you . . ."

Daisy listened to Jessee's words, but somehow they weren't making any sense. They banged and crashed around in her brain, but they didn't fit anywhere. They didn't settle in any spot so that she could understand them. All she knew was that today she was supposed to marry the red-headed boy. Suddenly she lunged forward, jerked the covers back, leaped out of bed, and raced across the house and out the door before Jessee, flouncing and talking steadily, realized what was happening. When she turned around, the bed was empty and the front door was banging shut.

As Daisy flew across the field in back of the house, heading toward the woods, her long, white flour-sack nightgown clinging to her legs, she heard Jessee screaming wildly for her to come back.

"I'll skin you alive, you little fool! Don't you do this to me, Daisy! You come back here, damn you!"

Daisy wouldn't stop! She wouldn't go back! Stickers and small, hard twigs on the ground cut into the soles of her feet, nettles scraped at her arms, but she wouldn't stop. She would run and run and run just the way Granny Henry said she should. She would run into forever and never stop!

At Toby's Creek, Daisy collapsed in the grass, pressing her cheeks into the fragrant dampness. Her temples thudded like a hammer and for a moment she couldn't get her breath into her lungs. But it came finally and she began to cry. Above her in the trees, birds gathered and stared down at her. Squirrels and field mice came close to observe. A frog on the bank of the creek called out to his mate and they croaked loudly to each other, singing a forlorn song. Even the frogs and the birds and the squirrels had a sameness, she thought. In all the world, people were alike. They looked the way they were supposed to look, acted the way they were supposed to act, and did the things they were supposed to do. Only *she* was different.

"Oh, Granny Henry, if only you was here, I wouldn't be so afraid!" she moaned into her hands. "I don't want to get married and I don't know what it all means! Granny . . . I'm so afraid!" Suddenly she remembered Terence and Grace tucked beneath a corner of her pillow. If only she had grabbed the envelopes before she ran out of the house, she thought, sniffing hard and wiping at her nose and eyes. Then she covered her face with her hands and whispered their two names into her palms.

Suddenly she stiffened. Someone was there, near her in the grass. She could feel the presence like a warm glow on her skin. Slowly she moved her hands down from her face and turned her head to look up, fearing that it might be Jessee or Delbert or even the red-headed boy.

"Why are you crying so, Daisy?" The voice was kind and soft and familiar.

The morning sun was behind the figure, so bright that he was darkened and Daisy could not see his face. He wore a long, flowing maroon-colored cape of velvet with the hood covering his head and shoes with heels and bright, shining buckles that caught the sun and made them seem to dance with golden lights. The strange shoes were familiar too.

"Terence!" Daisy gasped. But could it be Terence? she wondered. This was someone standing straight and tall, taller even than she was, and *not* a doll made out of paper. And yet . . . yet the voice was Terence's voice.

"You called my name, Daisy. I heard you," Terence said. "Grace is still sleeping. The little tousle-head never wakes without a good punch."

"It really *is* you," Daisy said, struck with awe and relief at the same time.

"I have something for you, Daisy," Terence said as he put his hand beneath his cape and drew out a small, very old, and worn-looking book. He handed it to Daisy.

Daisy stared at the book with eyes as wide as the sky and reached for it. "Granny Henry's book! Her poetry book! The one Uncle Flint and Aunt Lou took away!" She brought the book to her lips, kissed it, and hugged it to her breast. "How did you get it, Terence? Did Uncle Flint give it to you? No! He couldn't of give it to you! No . . . no . . . he couldn't of." Daisy got up, still clutching the book close, and stared into Terence's face. She could see it now, in the shadows of the hood, as handsome as he had been the first moment the paper doll agent had shown him to her.

Terence smiled warmly. "Seeing you happy makes me happy, Daisy."

But Daisy asked again, "How did you get Granny Henry's book?"

"It's not *how* I got it that matters. It only matters that you now have it, Daisy. It was one of your wishes. Don't you remember?" Terence said and Daisy frowned in deep puzzlement.

Everything was so strange, she thought. Terence, a paper doll, here with her, real and talking and alive and . . . and giving her Granny Henry's book of poems! There were a hundred questions in her mind, but before she could even begin to ask them, Terence stepped closer and said, "You didn't tell me why you were crying, Daisy."

Could she have forgotten in her joy over the book? she wondered. Suddenly all her fear and worry came rushing back into her like a storm. "This is the day I have to marry the red-headed boy," she answered, with a look of pain enveloping her face, and she pressed the book even closer to her heart. "The woman Jessee, my mama, says I have to."

A heavy, deep crease settled on Terence's brow. There was pain in his eyes. His smile went away. He stepped even closer to Daisy and touched her arm with his gloved hand. "Oh, Daisy. . . ," he began but he could say no more for suddenly Jessee's loud, angry yell split the air. Her footsteps were near. They could hear her stomping over the twigs and leaves, getting closer to them. And suddenly . . . suddenly she was there, reaching out for Daisy's arm, yanking and pulling and half dragging her away from the creek. Daisy looked all around for Terence. He was gone. As quickly as he had appeared, he was gone. She held the book of poems tightly in her arm, pressed against her chest. She couldn't let Jessee see it.

"You're coming with me, Daisy Flowerdew! Ain't no way you're going to get out of marrying Elmer Goots, so you just as well make up your mind to it!" Jessee panted as she drug and pulled the protesting Daisy into the field behind the house.

Daisy grumbled and moaned and kicked, trying to pull back, but Jessee overpowered her each time, hung onto her, and wouldn't let her go. By the time Jessee got her into the front yard, Daisy had gone limp, calmed down, and stopped trying to get free. When Jessee saw that she was no longer objecting, she put her arm around her and began to talk soothingly to her as they went up the steps.

"Now, honey, you know I wouldn't send you off into no lions' den ner nothing that would hurt you. You'll be just fine. Why, it won't be long and you'll have a little young'un all your own. You'll be married and have a family and you'll be as happy as you could ever think about being. You just come on in the house and I'll fix you up real sweet in that dress I give you." Jessee opened the door and they went inside the house.

In her room, while Jessee turned away to pick up the dress from a chair where she had laid it, Daisy quickly shoved the book under her mattress. When Jessee returned with the dress she said, "Now take off your gown, Daisy, so's we can get this dress on you."

Daisy, feeling resigned now to what lay ahead of her, did as she was told and stood before Jessee barefoot with her hair stringing in tangles to her waist. She looked at the floor, trembling and feeling imprisoned and lost.

"You'll see," Jessee said as she tossed the dress over Daisy's head and pulled it down neatly. "Everything will be just fine. Why, heck, every girl I ever heard of was nervous as a cat on her wedding day." She buttoned the dress and stood back to study Daisy. Well, she thought, it wouldn't matter what anyone did, Daisy never would look right. She never would look like a real, honest-to-goodness girl. She took Daisy's chin and tilted her face up so that Daisy looked directly into her eyes.

"I reckon a good face washing and hair combing is about all I can do for you," Jessee said and Daisy looked down. Jessee sighed and took her hand away. "I'm going to get my comb. While I'm gone, you put them shoes on over yonder by that chair." She nodded toward the scuffed, tan-colored high-heeled shoes with the little bows on them, then walked out of the room.

Daisy looked down at the dress she had on. It was

long and straight and ugly with great orange flowers on it that seemed to shout out, "LOOK AT ME!" The one thing she didn't want! The dress was an old one of Jessee's and it never would have fit Daisy if it hadn't been cut in a chemise style. She looked at the high heels. How was she ever going to walk in them? She had never walked in anything in her life but Uncle Flint's brogans and her own bare feet. But she had no time to think about the shoes and the dress. As soon as Jessee left the room, she went quickly to the bed and pulled the paper doll envelopes from the edge of her pillow. Her hands were shaking as she opened the envelope that belonged to Terence and nervously moved her fingers inside. Would he be there? she wondered. Had he really been at Toby's Creek with her or had she only imagined it? No, no . . . she couldn't have imagined it, because Granny Henry's book of poems was real and right here with her. Her fingers touched the pieces of paper inside the envelope and she pulled one out slowly.

"Terence!" Daisy breathed in amazement. He was here, in her hand, smiling up at her from his paper face! "Terence, how can you be here? How can you be *paper* again?" Daisy whispered desperately. But the paper face merely continued to smile at her exactly as it had before.

"Daisy, have you got them shoes on? Come out here in the front room and let me comb your hair. Delbert will be along any minute to take us to town. Hurry up now!" It was Jessee calling impatiently for her. Very quickly she placed Terence back into the envelope and pushed it under the pillow.

"Daisy!" Jessee yelled. "Did you hear me?"

Daisy hurried to push her feet down into the high-heeled shoes and wobbled unsteadily out of the room. Jessee was standing in the middle of the floor in the front room, a comb in her hand and a fretful look on her face.

"That hair of yourn is a rats' nest!" Jessee growled. "I ought to of cut it off a long time ago." Suddenly she reached out and grabbed the long, tangled tail of Daisy's hair and began to beat the comb down through it.

After what seemed an eternity of pain, Jessee had all the snarls and tangles out and Daisy's hair lay straight and long and flowing beyond her waist. Her head throbbed and her eyes were filled with tears. Jessee dropped the comb and put her arm around Daisy's shoulder.

"Don't cry, honey, this is your wedding day," she told her with a tight squeeze. "Now, let's go out on the porch and wait for Delbert. He ought to be here any minute."

As they walked out on the porch, Delbert was just pulling into the yard. He had left the store in the hands of Bobby Gene Williams, telling him he would be gone the rest of the day and only be back in time to close the store. He had looked forward to this day for a long time. Soon he would be all alone with Jessee again. He stopped the car and eyed Daisy critically. "If that ain't the most ridiculous sight I ever laid eyes on, I don't know what is!" he said out loud. Then he smiled at Jessee and and called out, "Guess what, hon?"

"What, honey bear?" Jessee called back as she took Daisy's hand and pulled her down the steps toward the car.

"Just as I was opening the store this morning, old man Howard from up on the hill come along. He'd just got off the train and walked over from the depot. He asked me if it was true what he'd heard about your girl going to marry Elmer Goots. I told him it was and he said to come up to his place when the ceremony was over and he'd give a little breakfast party for the newlyweds." Delbert threw his head back and laughed.

"Well, what's so funny, honeybee?" Jessee asked as she opened the car door and shoved Daisy in between her and Delbert.

"Who'd want to give a party for Daisy?" Delbert laughed again as he started up the car and drove away from the house.

Chapter
Seventeen

There was no courthouse in Vineyard Flats. Judge Santos Angelo held court in his home, where he also performed weddings and could be found most afternoons snoozing on the long black divan that sat along the wall near his desk. On the opposite side of the room were two short rows of hard-backed chairs and a spittoon. The judge's desk sat at the narrow end of the room, before a broad window that looked out over his wife's garden. Today, since he was performing a wedding, he had spiffed up in a new, crisp shirt, a brown neck tie, and his best dark jacket. He sat at his desk, his hands folded and his eyeglasses slipped down his nose just a little so that he could easily see over the top of them, as he waited for the wedding party to arrive.

The door clicked, opened, and Daisy walked in,

teetering unsteadily in the tan high heels, between Jessee and Delbert. Judge Angelo pushed his glasses up on his nose, stood up, and extended his hand across the desk to Delbert.

"Well . . . well . . . well . . . ," the judge said, eyeing Daisy over the roof of his glasses. He had heard about Daisy, but had never seen her. The child that stood before him, her eyes averted and her hands trembling against a small bouquet of forget-me-nots, was a peculiar sight, he thought. But no less peculiar than he had heard from gossip around town. Well, he decided, it was a shame, and the best he could do was to get the whole thing over with as soon as possible. Still, he wondered how even Elmer Goots, as lazy and no-account as he was, could marry such a child. Ten dollars sure carried a passel of power with it, he concluded as he let Delbert's hand go.

"This here is Jessee, my wife," Delbert said. "And this is her girl, Daisy Flowerdew."

"How do, ma'am." The judge nodded to Jessee and she smiled. He looked at Daisy again and she put her head down and stared at the tops of Jessee's shoes. They were stuck so tightly on her feet that large blisters had already formed on her heels. "Well, happy is the bride the sun smiles on," Judge Angelo said brightly and Jessee smiled again.

I remember you, the judge thought as he caught the wisp of Jessee's smile in his dark eyes. You was waiting tables over to Hoosier City when I went through there once. You was hooked up with some cowboy feller and he took off and left you flat with that girl,

Daisy Flowerdew. She don't look a thing like you. Tooken after that cowboy, I reckon. He cleared his throat, pushed his glasses up on his nose, and asked, "And where is the groom?"

"He'll be along," Delbert answered and to Jessee he whispered, "He'd *better* be along if he don't want that red-haired head of his pinched off at the elbows!"

Daisy kept her head down and wished with all her heart she could run away to Toby's Creek and be with Terence and Grace. She wondered again if Terence could have truly been *real*? Yes! The book of Granny Henry's poems was proof that he had been. Oh, if only he were here with her now!

Jessee moved closer to Daisy and whispered, "Hold your head up, honey. It don't look right for you to appear so glum on your wedding day."

Daisy refused to look up. She would never look up! They couldn't make her! They were selling her! *Selling* her just like Uncle Flint sold his sows at the county sales! Well, she wasn't a sow! If only she could make them think of her as a real and true girl! A real and true person with feelings and thoughts. But she knew she never could.

Jessee mashed her lips together and sighed disgustedly. Daisy was hopeless. Even on her wedding day she couldn't act normal. Delbert looked at the clock on the wall behind the rows of chairs on the other side of the room and shifted nervously from one leg to the other. It was three minutes past nine. He turned and glanced at the closed door behind him, then at Jessee. There was a worried frown on her face.

Delbert reached out and put his arm around her shoulder and tried to smile.

"Don't worry. That little cuss will be here, if he knows what's good for him," he said close to Jessee's ear. And, as he spoke, the door inched slowly open and Olive Goots, wearing a black dress and a black straw hat with purple grapes bobbing over the rim, came into the room. Her mouth was pinched up tight and her eyes were red-rimmed from crying. Behind her Elmer walked with his shoulders slumped and his eyes downcast. He wore his old clothes and old brogans and his hair was so topsy-turvy it looked like a stump full of granddaddy spiders had settled in it. He avoided Delbert's eyes and studied the floor as he approached Judge Angelo's desk. Olive gave Delbert and Jessee a savage, accusing look and shot her nose into the air.

Daisy slowly raised her eyes at the same time Elmer did and the two looked at each other for the first time. They stared at each other, each quaking inside, each horrified with the appearance of the other, each wishing they could escape from the other.

Olive Goots's eyes penetrated Daisy and she moaned out, "Oh, my poor boy! My poor Elmer!" Then she dropped her face into a handkerchief and sobbed loudly.

Judge Angelo gave Olive a sympathetic look and shoved his hand across his desk to Elmer. "How do, young man," he said as he pumped Elmer's hand. "I reckon we're all ready now." He dropped Elmer's hand and cleared his throat. "You young folks come and stand side by side in front of the desk," he said.

Jessee gave Daisy a quick, desperate look and whispered, "Step up there, honey."

Elmer looked at Olive for some kind of reassurance, but her face was still buried in her handkerchief. He shot Delbert a swift, fearful glance and Delbert made a threatening fist at his side. Elmer saw it and moved up to the desk.

The two, Elmer and Daisy, strangers in a strange place before a strange man, stood side by side now, quivering and near tears, wishing they had never laid eyes on each other. But it was too late for that. Words came in distant, meaningless waves of sound to Daisy. What was that old man with the drooping glasses and baggy suit saying to her? No . . . no! She wouldn't let her mind make sense of any of it! She wouldn't! But he had said her name! He was staring at her, waiting and studying her. She felt the sweat sizzling around the blisters on her heels, felt her palms grow damp.

"Judge . . . my girl can't talk," Jessee said in a tight, nervous voice and Daisy felt the words thunder all through her.

"Is she deaf and dumb?" Judge Angelo asked.

"She can understand some, but she ain't never talked, that I know of," Jessee answered uncomfortably.

"Well, then . . . let her nod her head," the judge said.

"Yes, sir," Jessee said and she touched Daisy's

shoulder and said in a low voice, "Now, Daisy, honey, whatever the judge asks you, you just nod your head up and down." Jessee looked back at the judge and said, "She understands now."

The words began again in their meaningless waves, plunging down through Daisy hot and fiery. Jessee nudged her arm and, like a puppet on a string, she nodded her head. The words started again and, beside her, she could feel Elmer falter, clear his throat, and croak out, "I reckon."

Suddenly her hand was lifted and she felt the crude scratch of a thin piece of wire being forced onto her finger, felt Elmer's sweaty skin against hers, and she jerked her hand away.

Delbert craned his neck to see the ring and sneered at the sight of the twisted wire. Judge Angelo stared at the wire with a puzzled frown. Olive Goots groaned and sobbed, and Jessee sighed with relief.

"You can go ahead and kiss your bride," Judge Angelo said and Daisy turned to glare hotly at Elmer, who backed away, frightened and embarrassed. "Well, you ain't the first shy couple I ever joined in marriage," the judge said gently.

Suddenly Delbert reached for Jessee and hugged her, and Olive grabbed Elmer and hung onto him tightly, crying into his shoulder. Then Jessee was beside Daisy, kissing her cheek and patting her shoulder, and Delbert was telling Jessee, "Thank the Lord *that* is over!" Daisy's head swam. She felt like she could throw up. Her insides trembled violently.

She glared at the horrible wire twisted around her finger.

Delbert went to shake Judge Angelo's hand. "Much obliged," he told him. Then he added, "Say, old man Howard is cooking up a breakfast for the newlyweds here, if you'd like to come. I know you'd be welcome. We're going up on the hill soon as we leave here."

"Well, that's mighty neighborly of you, Delbert, but the missus and I are going to Hoosier City to see my daughter's new baby. He's our first grandchild and we're mighty excited about seeing him." Judge Angelo raised his hand to his chin and scratched it. "You know, I've done give up on ever getting to do a wedding ceremony for them Howard sisters. They done got too old, I reckon. Ain't no one around these parts left to marry them. Everyone has already got hooked up." He chuckled and added, nodding toward Daisy and Elmer, "Least ways, them two has got youth on their side."

"Well, let's go," Delbert said loudly. "Old man Howard is putting on the feed bag for all of us!"

Olive pulled her head out of Elmer's shoulder and dabbed at her eyes with her flooded handkerchief. "Bart Howard? Up on the hill?"

"That's right," Delbert answered with a smile.

Olive turned back to Elmer and smiled. "Did you hear that, son? *Bart Howard* is having a party for us!" Olive had never been to the old mansion and she had never expected to be invited there. Suddenly her face broke into an even broader smile. She adjusted the grapes on her hat and patted down Elmer's shirt collar.

Everyone headed out of the judge's office, Olive and Elmer close together and Daisy wobbling along on the high heels between Jessee and Delbert. Outside, they all climbed into Delbert's car, Jessee in front with Delbert and Daisy in the back seat, hunched into the corner, setting next to Olive, and Elmer staring out the window on the other side of his mother. Daisy could hear Olive breathing heavily and, from the corner of her eyes, she could see her thin chest rise and fall beneath her black dress.

Suddenly Olive turned to Daisy and snarled, "If that piece of old wire on your finger was a real ring, I'd bend it in two with a pair of wire pliers. And your finger right along with it!"

Daisy nudged herself even closer into the corner of the car seat. She tried to pretend she wasn't in the car, but it did no good. She *was* in it and she *was* setting next to Olive Goots and she *was* now married to Elmer Goots! If only she could jump out of the window or the car door! If only she could run away and away and away, just like Granny Henry said she should!

The car headed onto the hill road and climbed up slowly, grumbling and chugging as it heaved along. The wire on Daisy's finger pinched and she wished she could take it off and pitch it out the window. If Granny Henry were here, she would rub her finger with lots of soap suds and the wire would slip right off. If Granny Henry were here, she would have told Olive Goots to shut her mouth and not speak to Daisy in such a way! If Granny Henry were here . . .

Daisy sighed forlornly and pushed her folded fist over her mouth. The car reached the top of the hill and curved around to the front of the old weather-beaten mansion and her heart began to pound wildly.

Chapter
Eighteen

The first thing Daisy saw as the car reached the top of the hill was the wilted, flowering shrubbery close to the mansion, and the wisteria vines that looped and crawled and sagged like a giant snake all across the long veranda. She noticed, too, that the great lofty house itself seemed to be wilted. Its roof slumped and curved and the once white paint was now a faded, chipped gray.

As the car got closer to the mansion, Daisy's eyes fell upon three women who stood on the yellowed grass beside a clump of rosebushes. The roses hung limply over the dry leaves, wilting from thirst, their colors looking as old and faded as the women who stood near them. But, Daisy thought, the women were pretty, too. Their sheer pastel-colored dresses rippled against them as they moved and their hair was swept up on their heads and held by combs with stones that glittered and winked in the sunlight. Pleasant smiles curved the lips on their homely faces and they seemed to be excited to see the car approaching.

"Oh, looky yonder!" Olive Goots cried, leaning across Elmer to peer out the car window. "Ain't that the Howard girls?" She pointed at them with her finger.

"That's them," Elmer said.

"But they look so *old*," Olive said with a frown of disappointment.

Elmer chuckled. "They is old, Ma. But they ain't as old as you."

Olive snorted and raised her hand in a wave to the sisters and all three waved back in a friendly way. But their eyes were on Elmer.

"Wave, Elmer!" Olive said, punching him in his arm, and Elmer lifted his hand and waved without enthusiasm.

"Wonder why them girls never married?" Olive questioned.

"I wouldn't exactly call them 'girls,'" Jessee said from the front seat. "Look at them double chins and that gray hair and they ain't got a sign of a waist on them."

Delbert drove past the waving sisters and pulled to a stop in front of the house just as Bart Howard appeared on the veranda beneath the dripping wisteria. His face glowed with warmth and friendliness as he came down the steps and walked to the car. "Welcome! Welcome all!" he said with a flourish as he raised both hands in the air.

Delbert got out of the car and shook hands with

Bart as the sisters came running up from the lawn and opened the doors for Jessee and Elmer to climb out of the car. Elmer stood beside the car while Olive and Jessee got out and exchanged chatter and smiles with the sisters. Soon the doors were slammed shut and it wasn't until everyone had started walking toward the house that Jessee remembered Daisy and turned to stare into the window of the car.

"Oh . . . Daisy!" Jessee said and all at once everyone stopped walking and looked back at Daisy too.

Daisy's head was down, her eyes studying the ugly wire wound around her finger, but she knew they were all standing there before the veranda steps, their heads turned, staring in the car at her. She could always tell when someone was staring at her. Her stomach would churn and her heart pound fearfully, wondering what would happen to her if she suddenly looked up into the eyes of strangers.

All at once the car door was jerked open and Jessee, leaning down, hissed in a low voice. "Don't just set there like that, Daisy!"

Daisy looked up, startled, feeling her heart pound in her throat and in her temples. Jessee's pretty face was all red. "Come *on*, Daisy!" She reached for Daisy's wrist and pulled, but Daisy pulled back, farther into the seat. "Damn your hide, anyway!" Jesse exploded. "You better come out of there! Don't you set there and embarrass me in front of the Howards! This party is for *you*!" Jessee's white hair fell across her face as her words shook out of her mouth. She gave another hard, quick yank and Daisy fell forward.

She tried to pull back again, but Jessee held onto both her wrists, refusing to let go. "Damn you! Damn you!" she sputtered as she pulled, and her saliva spewed out of her mouth and all over Daisy's face.

Finally, Jessee got her out of the car and shoved her up against the side of it. Daisy felt her back thud against it and felt the pain all the way down her legs and into her feet, where the high-heeled shoes had cut into her skin. She could hear the Howard sisters whispering about her, could hear their chitters and giggles as all six eyes moved critically over her. She felt as though the ugly flowers on her dress were all that was covering her, as though the rest of the dress had been stripped away from her except for those huge, ugly orange flowers. Suddenly the flowers were curling all around her, tighter and tighter, trying to suffocate her!

The Howard sisters, Elmer and Olive Goots and Delbert were all laughing at her, whispering behind their hands, running their eyes up and down her. She *knew* they were! Now her breath would not come! Her heart pounded and thudded and ripped at her chest and her breath would not come! If only her legs would move! If only she could run!

Jessee gave her a little shove. "Now you come on!" she hissed exasperatedly through a faked smile as she patted at Daisy's hair and pretended to adjust the shoulder of the hideous dress. Somehow Daisy began to clop along, weaving uncertainly and almost falling as her ankle twisted and turned in the high-heeled shoes. Above the sound of her heart pounding in her ears, she could hear the mocking giggles of the Howard sisters as they watched her stumbling toward them. Jessee, walking very close at her side, jabbed her in her arm and said through her faked smile, "Look *up*!"

Reluctantly, Daisy raised her head and her eyes met Bart Howard's eyes and found unexpected kindness there. He came forward, stretching out his hand, and said, "Welcome, little bride. Welcome."

"Smile!" Jessee demanded through her smile. But Daisy's tightly clenched mouth could not rise into a smile, even for this new, kind voice. It was as frozen as her face.

Everyone began walking up the steps of the veranda and moved to one end, where the wisteria vines and the lavender-colored flowers made a colorful canopy above a large table with a lace cloth and china and crystal that glimmered with sunlit speckles. On each side of the table and at each end were tall, hardbacked chairs with soft cushions, waiting to be set in. Across from the table, against the wall of the house, stood another, longer table that held so much food it seemed to sink in the center. There were two pans of golden-topped biscuits and covered dishes of steaming gravy, sausages, and bacon that made the air smell good and brownish-colored hotcakes under a glass dome, a large platter of fried eggs with orange centers, china pots of preserves and syrup, jugs of milk and orange juice, hot coffee and cream and sugar and a little round bowl of toothpicks all spread out like a fan.

"Glory be!" Olive Goots exclaimed when she saw the long table of food. "I ain't never seen so much food except after a funeral!"

Jessee and Delbert glanced at each other with approving smiles as their eyes sped along the table of food. Elmer, whose eyes had grown wide with pleasure, couldn't keep from smacking his lips in hungry anticipation and exclaiming, "Boy-howdy! Look at that!"

The Howard sisters giggled and rushed around, pulling out chairs for everyone to sit in.

Daisy was placed at the end of the table, across from Jessee and Delbert and beside Bart Howard. On the other side of her two chairs were vacant. Beside them, Elmer sat with his ragged shirtsleeves visible as he rested his elbows on the table. Olive sat across from Elmer, her weeping sadness now replaced by a bright, cheerful expression. The chair at the very end of the table would be taken by one of the sisters.

Bart Howard had not let on to anyone that he thought it strange the newly married young couple did not even set next to each other at the table or how they seemed so totally distant in mind and spirit. Nor had he let on how odd he thought the young bride looked. Never in his life had he seen such a strange-looking creature as this Daisy. Her face was tomboyish, without a trace of femininity. And her eyes—peculiar catlike eyes with flickers of yellow in them—were shifty. Denoting a suspicious nature, perhaps? he wondered. Or was it fear? He could not be sure. She seemed to be looking up from under her eyelashes now, those catlike eyes darting in all directions at once. Her hands sat nervously in her lap beneath the table, but he had already seen the crude piece of wire that curled around her finger. The dress she wore must have come straight from Miss Minnie's barn sale. And the shoes! He would have chuckled on first sight of the girl swaying and wobbling, tilting this way and that on the tall stiltlike shoes, if she had not been such a pitiful sight.

The girl's mother is pretty enough, Bart thought, as his eyes left Daisy and shifted to Jessee. There definitely was something pleasing about her. But Elmer's mother, old Olive Goots. . . . Well, never mind, he decided, dismissing the thoughts as rapidly as they had come.

The three sisters moved around the table chatting pleasantly as they poured hot coffee into cups and milk and orange juice into the crystal glasses.

"This here is better than a café, ain't it?" Delbert remarked to Jessee. She nodded her head and thought, better than that café in Hoosier City. There sure weren't no tablecloths there, only them bare wood tables and the counter with cigarette burns in it. There weren't no fine china neither.

The sisters had taken all the plates to the long table against the wall to fill them. Soon they began bringing them back and placing them before everyone, filled to overflowing.

"This here is fair about a feast!" Elmer said with delight as Ivy set a plate before him.

"The girls prepared every little nibble all by themselves," Bart said proudly, speaking of the "girls" as though they were not grown women.

"Well, they is to be complimented," Olive said, beaming over her plate. The sisters turned to smile at her and to thank her.

At last, everyone was served . . . except Daisy. Bart noticed and turned to frown over at his three daughters, who now stood at the long table, their backs to everyone, giggling and whispering secretively.

"But, girls . . . you have forgotten the most important guest of all," Bart told them, glancing toward Daisy. Her head was down, staring into the lacy curlicues of the tablecloth. Everyone at the table was talking and did not seem to notice Daisy had not been served.

Ivy turned her head and said, "Don't worry, Papa. Sisters and I would never forget the bride. We're preparing a *very special* plate for her." She turned back to the food and Irene and Irma spoke in unison, *"A very special plate."* Suddenly all three heads sprang together and they began giggling again.

"Very well, then," Bart said and, turning to Daisy, he said, "Only a moment more, my dear." Then he turned back to Delbert, who had been mentioning several items in the dry goods store that interested the old man.

No one seemed to notice the three sisters glance around and give Daisy narrow-eyed, contemptuous sneers or hear their vicious whispers about her. While everyone else began to eat, Bart excused himself and went into the house to place a record on the Victrola.

Before he was back, a beautiful Strauss waltz drifted out onto the veranda. The sound swirled through the tangled vines of the wisteria and mixed with their fragrance and the smell of the food.

"Ah," Bart said, settling comfortably into his chair and closing his eyes briefly to the sound of the lively music. "How quickly melodies make one recall pleasantries of the past." And, turning to Jessee, he asked, "Don't you find that to be true, Miz Heath?"

"Yes," Jessee answered. "Every time I hear Hank Williams sing 'Your Cheatin' Heart' I think about old use-to-be days."

"'Your Cheatin' Heart'? Is that the one that goes, 'It will tell on you'?" Bart asked with an eyebrow raised.

"That's the one," Jessee answered. "It just always does something to me. It makes me feel . . . well, I can't hardly explain it."

Bart reached over and patted the top of Jessee's hand. "I know just what you mean, Miz Heath. Indeed I do. Long-ago times haunt us all."

Haunt—yes, that's a good word to use, Jessee thought. For, every time she heard that song, she was haunted by the memories of those awful times in Hoosier City when Daisy was little and they were half starved and—and her daddy went away and . . .

Jessee stared across the table at Daisy, whose head was still down, and silently thanked God that now the girl was married and she could relax and breathe easy. When Flint and Lou had first brought her to Vineyard

Flats, she was sure her world was over, sure her marriage to Delbert was doomed. Jessee took in a deep, relieved breath that everything had worked out. She let the sound of the waltz flutter around in her head and began to keep time to it with her feet under the table.

Chapter Nineteen

Daisy was tapping her feet too. The quick, heady sound of the waltz seemed to float right into her, sending a pleasurable sensation all the way down to her feet. For a moment, just for a moment, she felt she was being lifted away and away and away by the music. It was such a wonderful feeling that she almost forgot her self-consciousness and was not aware of Bart watching her.

Poor, homely child, Bart thought and his eyes flickered from Daisy to Elmer, who was engrossed in conversation with his mother. If only you would give some attention to your bride, speak to her, look at her . . . He sighed deeply, almost angrily, knowing that Elmer would do none of those things. But suddenly, as the music swelled like rippling ocean waves around them, Bart stood up and went to Daisy. He touched the back of her chair and said, "My dear child, I haven't danced with a new bride for years. Won't you give me the pleasure?"

Daisy's head rose, her eyes flashed up into the old, kind blue eyes of Bart Howard, and her heart trembled. "D-dance. . . ?" her heart drummed fearfully.

"Come, child," Bart said and he took her hand and pulled her gently from the chair and guided her to the other end of the long veranda. "Let us dance together. Let us shine on your day as brightly as the noonday sun."

At first Daisy stumbled awkwardly in Jessee's high heels. At first her heart thundered so that she could hardly breathe. And at first her whole body quaked with fear. She knew everyone was watching her. She could hear the Howard sisters giggling, the harsh sound cutting right through the music. She could hear Elmer snicker and saw him slap his knee with the flat of his hand. She heard Olive say, "Ain't that a sight!" as her hot, scowling eyes ran up and down her. Oh! I'm going to die! Daisy thought dizzily.

"That old man's got a kind heart," Jessee said to Delbert as they watched with wide eyes how Bart Howard took Daisy into his arms and began to move her across the floor.

"He'd have to have, to dance with that dummy!" Delbert snorted.

Suddenly Daisy's feet went light as a feather. Jessee's high heels stopped pinching and her blisters stopped burning. All at once a radiant luminescence appeared around her ugly dress, and within the blink of an eye it was transformed into a beautiful gown of the palest blue chiffon that fluttered and swayed as she moved along the floor.

"Shine! Shine, little Daisy!" Bart whispered to Daisy with a broad smile on his face and his blue eyes twinkling. *"Shine!"* And all at once he whirled her round and round and her chiffon gown went flying out in a circle around her and her long hair rose and jumped and spun around her shoulders.

Daisy danced with Bart now as though she had always danced, as though she knew every step, as though . . . as though she were not Daisy Flowerdew at all, but some beautifully gowned new girl who had entered Daisy's body and was telling her exactly what to do. Even her face had changed and now held a soft, bright prettiness that it had never had before this moment.

The Howard sisters stood glaring jealously with their eyes popping and their mouths hanging open as they watched their father move Daisy gracefully up and down the veranda. Jessee and Delbert, Elmer and Olive stared with disbelieving, thunderstruck expressions on their faces.

Time seemed to stop, as though some unseen stranger had appeared and taken their picture, catching them forever wearing their masks of amazement. Even the wisteria was still. No small draft blew onto the veranda. Not even the food grew cold. It stayed as warm as when the Howard sisters had first served it.

Our little wilting Daisy has finally bloomed, Bart said to himself as up and down and all around the veranda they moved, keeping time to the lilting music.

Daisy closed her eyes for only a moment, opened them, and the music suddenly stopped. Her feet began to ache and her blisters burned. She looked down at her dress. It was the same ugly dress of Jessee's with the horrible garish flowers. It was all over, whatever it had been, that had made her so wonderfully happy.

"Well," Bart said when he returned Daisy to her chair at the table, amid the hostile stares, "it is indeed a pleasure to have all of you here on such a happy occasion." He looked around the table. "I'd like to, as we partake of this delicious breakfast my girls have prepared, make a toast to the bride and groom." He went to the cupboard beneath the long table where the food was held and pulled a bottle of wine from it. He returned to the table holding the bottle up and said, "This bottle of wine was made from grapes grown on this very land close to seventy years ago. Pass your glasses down this way so that I can fill them."

Everyone began to speak at once and to pass their glasses to the end of the table, where the old man, who had opened the bottle with a proud flourish, poured the red wine into each glass. When he had finished and the glasses were sent back along the table, he raised his glass and said, "To the newly married young couple." He stopped and looked at Daisy and smiled. "May they live in happiness ever after this day."

Bart did not notice, as he tilted the glass to his lips,

the sullen, jealous, penetrating looks his daughters directed toward Daisy or that they raised their glasses without drinking from them. Nor did he notice how Olive narrowed her eyes hatefully over the girl. But he did notice that Elmer drank down his glass of wine quickly and that Daisy did not even reach for her glass. It was only Delbert and Jessee who toasted the marriage joyously and with a great deal of relief.

Chapter Twenty

"And here is a *very special* bride's place *just for you*," Ivy said as she came to the table and set a plate down in front of Daisy and patted her shoulder. To Daisy, Ivy's touch felt like the sting of a yellow jacket.

Ivy hurried to the end of the table to sit next to Elmer, but just as she was ready to sit down, Irma grabbed the chair and plopped down into it. Ivy's face flushed with rage as she glared at the winning sister. She was compelled to sit next to Daisy, for Irene had already taken the chair on the other side of Elmer.

Everyone ate now with relish, talking and mumbling with delight over the delicious food, and complimenting the three sisters. Ivy, Irma, and Irene accepted the compliments with bright faces and shining smiles. But it was to Elmer that they looked for words of praise. None came. He was too busy gorging down everything in sight.

"Pick up your fork and eat!" Jessee mouthed at Daisy from across the table. "Don't embarrass me like this!"

Daisy, looking up from beneath her eyelashes, winced as she watched Jessee form the words on her lips. Slowly she reached for the fork beside her plate, picked it up with trembling fingers, and started to eat the fried egg that lay like a large sunflower in her plate. Suddenly her eyes grew wide. Her tongue burned with the taste of salt. The Howard girls, who had been watching her intently, began to giggle among themselves.

"Now, try that sausage!" Olive said to no one in particular through a mouth filled with food.

"Go on!" Jessee mouthed the words again and Daisy slid the fork down across the sausage, cutting it in two, and brought a piece to her mouth, forcing herself to chew and chew. Her mouth began to salivate with a taste like burning acid. It attacked her tongue, her gums, the roof of her mouth, her throat. The sausage was salted seven times over! Suddenly, she lunged her hand in the direction of the wine glass next to her plate, grabbed it, spilling half of it on the tablecloth, brought it to her mouth, and gulped at it. She swallowed, but the awful mixture of sweet wine and salt would not settle in her stomach. It lurched round and round, slapping and gurgling like the water and old clothes in Granny Henry's wringer washer always did. She looked up quickly from beneath her eyelashes and saw the hard, contemptuous gaze of the three Howard sisters. When they realized that she was looking at them, evil smiles of satisfaction spread across their lips. *They* had done this to her! *They* had done it deliberately!

Daisy's stomach lurched again as she felt the hot sting of salt rising in her throat, up . . . up . . . higher and higher until she knew, *she knew* she was going to throw up! Suddenly, wildly, she jumped up, knocking her chair back, and ran from the veranda with her mouth buried in her hands. Down the steps she flew and around the corner of the house.

Jessee jumped up and raced down the steps behind her. "Daisy!" she shouted, the red look of embarrassment shrouding her face. She rounded the corner of the house and saw Daisy leaning against the wall, her face an agonized ghostly white. "What is *wrong* with you?" Jessee's words were high and shrill.

Daisy raised her eyes to Jessee. The sun was hot on her face and in her eyes and the salt stung inside her nostrils and her throat and her brain spun in red and orange circles making her stomach ache and jolt even more. Sweat rose in her skin and rolled over her like fat drizzling over the sides of a scalding skillet.

Daisy could only stare helplessly at the sunspots that drove out of her brain and shot round and round on her mother's face. All at once someone else was there in the red and orange sunspots, spinning round and round with Jessee.

"Couldn't take the wine, eh, young lady?" It was Bart Howard's voice coursing toward her in a friendly chuckle. "Here, drink this. It will make you feel better." He handed her a glass of something cool and fizzy-sounding with little red and yellow and orange bubbles soaring up out of the liquid. "Come, come, now. Swallow it down. It can't hurt you. It will make you feel better," Bart went on, ordering her gently.

Daisy's fingers curled around the cool glass and she brought it to her mouth without spilling any of it. The waterfall of liquid rolled down her throat, soothing it and dissolving the burning sensation. When the glass was empty Bart took it from her and patted her shoulder, and the circling, colored sunspots left her eyes and Jessee stopped spinning.

"She'll be better by and by," Bart said to Jessee and, as he spoke, the three Howard sisters appeared. When he saw them he added, "My girls will stay with Daisy until she recovers completely. They've taken care of me many times in similar circumstances." He reached out and took Jessee's hand and placed it over his arm. "Let us continue with the music and the good food and the wine, my dear."

Relief flooded Jessee's face as though she were glad to be rescued from a distressing predicament. She walked away on the arm of the old man.

Chapter
Twenty-one

The Howard sisters stood in a half circle, surveying Daisy, their haughty stares pinning her to the wall of the house. Hatred glittered savagely in their cold eyes. The look was not unfamiliar to Daisy. She had seen it from others all her life and knew it well.

"You think you're really something, marrying Elmer Goots, don't you!" Ivy spat in an angry, accusing voice.

"And dancing with our papa!" Irene added.

Daisy gazed fearfully up at the sisters from beneath her eyelashes. Her steady gaze only served to make them more angry. Suddenly Irma reached out and yanked at the skirt of her dress as though she were pulling one of the huge ugly flowers out of it. "Look at this old dress, will you, sisters?" The girls laughed and the echo of their laughter bruised the air.

"The dress isn't half as bad as the shoes!" Irene said and all three laughed and looked down at the high heels and Daisy's feet, which had swollen painfully over the tight edges.

As they laughed, Ivy gave the skirt a hard, swift yank and the sound of the fabric ripping was as loud as the sound of glass shattering in a quiet room. Irma grabbed Daisy's wrist and yanked her hand up.

"Look at this ring, sisters! Did you ever *see* such a *diamond* in your born days?" she asked.

The sisters crowed and cackled with laughter, laughter that whirled round and round, up to the tree-tops, and soared overhead, shuddering into the air like some strange and fearful bird.

"It *had* to of cost a *fortune!*" Irene taunted.

"Only the *best* for such a *beautiful* bride!" Ivy sneered.

Finally Irma let go of Daisy's wrist and let it slam into her side. The laughter rattled on until Daisy felt the sound would explode inside her head. She edged farther into the splintery wall, feeling it scratch her bare arms. On her feet she could feel the tiny crawling sensation of ants. She must be standing on an ant hill! Ants were in the high heels, nosing between her toes, traveling up her ankles and legs. If only she could slap them away!

Irene's face, old and wrinkled and mottled, moved close to Daisy's face. The lines themselves seemed to speak hatefully into Daisy's eyes. She tried to look away, but she could not.

"You're not a *real* girl!" Irene said and her voice

was as hard and as deep as the lines on her face and as cold as the venom in her eyes.

Ivy moved closer. "The *only* reason Elmer Goots married you is because he was *paid* to!"

The three sisters moved back a little, watching Daisy's face closely, as though they expected shock and surprise to spread across it. But when it did not come, that angered them even more.

"You're just an ugly old freak!" Irene blasted hotly into her face. "Why don't you go off and join a freak show in a circus?"

As the sisters taunted her, the ants bit savagely into Daisy's flesh, and she brought her teeth hard into her lips so that she would not cry out. Oh, if only the Howard girls would go away! If only they would leave her alone! She closed her eyes, feeling more bites from the ants, and suddenly Ivy's hand was in her hair, pulling at it.

"Rag mop!" Ivy cried. "Rag mop! Rag mop!"

"Pull it harder!" Irma crowed. "Make her cry!"

Daisy's eyes flashed open. But she would not cry. She would not!

"She hasn't got a voice!" Ivy said, looking at Daisy peculiarily.

"She has a voice! She's just too stubborn to use it!" Irene said.

"Where? Where is your voice, old rag mop?" Ivy demanded, leaning close and squinting her eyes angrily into Daisy's face.

"Down her gullet!" Irene said and she sputtered with laughter.

"Let's see!" Irma said and suddenly her hand plunged into Daisy's mouth. All at once Daisy's teeth went crashing down into Irma's fingers. Irma screeched as loud as a wild animal.

"She bit me!" she shouted, yanking her hand away and holding her folded fist with her other hand. "She bit me!"

"Bit you?" Ivy cried indignantly.

"Who do you think you are to bite our sister?" Irene demanded and in an unexpected flash, the three sisters began to pummel Daisy, to slap her and shove her back and forth against the hard, splintery wall of the house. Daisy moaned in helpless agony, trying to hold her hands over her face.

"If it weren't for your stepfather bribing Elmer to marry you, he would be proposing to me right now!" Ivy puffed out between blows.

"You!" Irene exploded as she turned away from Daisy. "Elmer was going to marry *me*! Not you!"

"Fools, both of you!" Irma spit with her hands on her hips, leaning forward with her chin pushed out. "Elmer Goots was going to marry me!"

All at once, Daisy was forgotten as the three sisters argued and began to flash out at each other with their angry fists. This was Daisy's chance! Her chance to run and run and run like Granny Henry had said she should! With a great heave away from the wall, she charged away from the house, away from the fighting sisters, and ran like a bolt of lightning down into the back vineyard where the dead and gnarled grape stumps stood. She ran so quickly, so desperately, that she could not keep her balance in the high heels and abruptly went sprawling face first into the clotted ground.

But there was no time to lie there or to cry out. She jumped up, beating at the ants that still clung to her skirt and legs, kicked off the high-heel shoes, and ran like she had never run before, with her hair flying wildly behind her.

Chapter
Twenty-two

It seemed to Daisy that a whole eternity had passed before she reached Delbert's place on Dogtown Road. She had run until her breath was a painful gasp, until her bleeding feet left little balls of blood in the dirt road and her heart was only a tiny whimpering patter inside her chest. But still she ran and did not stop until she reached Toby's Creek, where she fell on her stomach with her legs and arms spread out and her hair tossed around her head like a broad, open fan.

All around Daisy, the birds and squirrels, the field mice and frogs watched with their eyes wide and curious, wondering what had happened to her. Everything was still and quiet except for her anguished cries. But somehow, with her crying, her breath came back into her lungs and her heart began to beat normally. After a while, the frogs along the creek started to croak out messages to one another and soon birds were relaying them from tree to tree. The squirrels and field mice ran about, all in a dither of activity.

They were all aware, before Daisy, that someone had appeared and stood near her. But soon she, too, felt the presence and her crying abruptly stopped. She rolled over and jumped up, ready to run again.

"Don't be afraid, Daisy! It's me, Terence!"

"Terence!" Daisy gasped and her look of fear turned into a flood of relief.

"Daisy, I wanted to stop that wedding! I could feel your pain as though it were my own, but I couldn't get out of that dratted envelope. Your pillow was so heavy it was like a house setting on top of me! I couldn't wake up Grace to help me, but finally I was able to inch my way out a leg and an arm at a time. I came as quickly as I could, Daisy. Oh, Daisy, I wasn't there to *help* you!" Sorrow was etched into Terence's handsome young face.

Daisy dropped back into the grass, too filled with emotion to stand any longer. Terence sat down beside her. "I'm so sorry, Daisy," he repeated. "If *only* I could have helped you . . ."

It was a strange feeling to have Terence setting so close to her, Daisy thought. He was so big now, bigger than she was. "My heart must of called for you," she said in a low, raw-from-crying voice. Then, looking deeply into his eyes, she added, "Your name is . . . is magic."

"Yes," Terence said softly. "But not magic enough

to have kept you from marrying that awful bump-kin."

"It ain't your fault, Terence," Daisy said. "No one could of stopped that wedding. Delbert would of took his whip to anyone that tried."

"It was one of your wishes, Daisy." Terence's voice was low and sad. He looked deeply into Daisy's eyes. "But I'll make it up to you. I promise that I will, Daisy."

"Ain't nothing you can do, Terence."

"Don't *say* that! You wait and see, I'll do some-thing."

"I wish . . . I just wish I was dead like Granny Henry."

"I know how you feel . . ."

"Ain't no one knows!"

"How do you think I feel being banished into a piece of paper? Do you think that is any kind of life, being a *paper doll boy*? It wasn't until Yule, the old paper doll agent, brought me to you that I was able to come to life as I have. *You* gave me life, Daisy. And you gave it to Grace." Daisy stared at Terence un-comprehendingly. "Don't you see, Daisy? If you hadn't believed in Grace and me, we would still just be drawings on a sheet of paper."

Daisy frowned. Her mind could not fathom what Terence was telling her and she still could not believe that he was here with her, talking to her, and yet . . . Grace and he had both talked with her. It was all too much of a mystery to her. Her thoughts and feelings seemed not to be her own, but belonged to Terence as well. Her eyes moved over his kind, handsome face. Terence moved closer to her and as he did, the wide maroon cape he wore spilled around them, enclosing them. Daisy reached up and touched his cheek, and at the same time he touched her hair. A chill ran through her. His fingers in her hair were like a kiss upon her lips.

A calm, almost perfect peace surrounded Daisy and Terence as they sat close together in the grass and for the first time since Granny Henry had died, Daisy felt a glow of warmth and security. But the peace and warmth of that secure feeling was soon broken by the harsh, insistent sound of Jessee yelling her name up to high heaven. Daisy's heart skipped. She looked into Terence's eyes and found sadness there. The loud calling got closer, so close that Daisy could feel the vibration of Jessee's footsteps in the ground under her.

Terence jumped up, pulling the hood of the maroon cape over his head. "I've got to hurry, Daisy, before she finds us together!" He grabbed Daisy's hand and pulled her up. "I'll never let you down again. I'll be back to help you. I promise. Just call for me." Then he was gone, sweeping away through the trees into the shadows of the day.

"Here you are!" Jessee cried furiously and she stomped across the grass and yanked Daisy by her arm. The look on her face was of anger and disgust and, yes, Daisy thought, even hatred. She tried to pull back and away, but Jessee had such a grip on her that she couldn't break free.

"The very idea of you running off like that! Away

from folks that went out of their way to have a fine wedding breakfast for you and your new husband!" Jessee went on.

But you don't understand, Daisy wanted to cry out. You don't know how I feel ner why I ran away ner anything about me! You ain't like Granny Henry. You're like everyone else. Like Delbert and everyone. Always thinking wrong things about me, always making me feel stupid and calling me stupid and treating me stupid, like I didn't have no thoughts ner feelings ner anything! The words and sentences falling over each other in her brain would not come out in her voice. She stared at Jessee, desperately trying to tell her everything with her eyes, but Jessee only continued to shout and pull at her.

"Come on, you're not getting away from me now, Daisy Goots!" Jessee yelled as she yanked furiously at Daisy.

Daisy Goots! No, no, I'm not Daisy Goots! I'm Daisy Flowerdew! Daisy Flowerdew, the name Granny Henry give me.

"You're married now!" Jessee went on screeching. "And you can't spend time hiding around Toby's Creek no more. You got to face up to the responsibilities of being a married woman."

Daisy tried to pull back again, but Jessee reached around and slapped her resoundingly across her face. It was such a hard blow that Daisy was knocked backward for a moment. "I am sick and tired of you, Daisy! I got my own life to live!" Jessee began to cry as she shouted and the tears washed down her cheeks in great wet blobs. "You don't know how it felt to know a man like your daddy. To wait and wonder when he left if he'd be coming back. You don't know what I went through being alone and having you in my belly and being afraid every day of my life. Afraid and alone!"

Jessee stopped and swiped at the tears on her cheeks and sniffed loudly. "Well . . . I ain't alone no m-more, Daisy. If only I could make you understand!" Jessee cried out helplessly.

Daisy hung her head and began to follow Jessee obediently now, allowing her to pull her along by her limp arm through the grass and sticker patches on the ground, away from the creek. She watched the dirty, sore, blood-smeared toes of her feet and whimpered. But Jessee was whimpering too.

"Oh, hon, I didn't aim to haul off and slap you. God knows I didn't want to slap you, not on your wedding day," Jessee said without turning her head to look at Daisy. She stared straight ahead as though she were talking to some unseen ghost of a person. "And it ain't that I don't care about you—I do care about you. It's just . . . you got to understand, I ain't going to let you ner no one else interfere with my life." Jessee tossed her head back, ending with a strong sound of finality in her voice.

The two walked silently, except for their sniffles, and when they neared the house Jessee cleared her throat and said, "Your new husband is up at the house waiting to take you home with him."

Daisy made noises of fear and protest way down

deep in the tunnel of her throat and tried to pull her arm free of Jessee's grip. But Jessee hung on, pulling like a plow horse until she had Daisy across the yard and stumbling up the front steps of the house. Unexpectedly, Daisy reached out with her free arm and looped it around the porch post, hanging on for dear life. Jessee pulled and pulled, but she could not make Daisy budge from her desperate hold on the post.

"DELLLLBERRRRRT!" Jessee exploded. "DELLLL-BERRRRT!"

The front door of the house sprang open and Delbert rushed forward, grabbing Daisy's hand and prying it, finger by finger, away from the post. Daisy, sobbing and kicking wildly, trying to break free, felt herself being abruptly lifted up across Delbert's shoulder, carried through the door of the house, and plunked down on her feet before a grinning Elmer Goots.

Chapter
Twenty-three

"She's all roostered up, but she's here," Delbert told Elmer after he had deposited Daisy before him.

Elmer's grin grew broader and his eyes glittered as he looked Daisy up and down like he'd just bought a good sow at a cheap price. What with the wedding breakfast at the Howards' and all the wine he had drunk, the girl that stood before him didn't look half so bad as she had when they had stood before Judge Angelo that morning. He had to chuckle to himself. He sure wasn't getting much in the way of a real girl for that ten dollars. But Ma ought to get some good work out of her in the pea patch and the house, he thought.

Daisy hung her head, feeling Elmer's eyes move over her. She was trapped with Elmer Goots standing in front of her, Delbert behind her, and Jessee beside her.

"Now, Daisy, ain't no call for you to go locking horns with your new husband," Delbert said. "You ought to get off your high horse so's you can get started off on the right foot."

Jessee moved closer to Daisy and put her arm around her. "Things will be just fine. You'll see. Now you go along with your husband. I got your things in a satchel for you and I'll bring them to Miz Goots's place tomorrow," she said. Then she moved even closer to Daisy and whispered, "You do everything your husband tells you to do so's you won't have no problems."

Daisy made a quick, desperate lurch toward the door, but Elmer grabbed her around her waist, picked her up, tossed her over his shoulder, and carried her out the door in the same way Delbert had carried her in. He went down the steps into the yard with Daisy's long hair sweeping the ground like broom straws and her fists hammering his back. But Elmer only grinned to himself and kept walking. Suddenly Daisy raised her head and bit hard into Elmer's thigh! He yelped loudly, dropped her to the ground, and leaned over to touch the sore spot. Daisy jumped up and shot away, running like the wind, but all at once Delbert was on the steps of the house sending out a circle of rope, looping it around her waist and pulling her back, gawking and struggling, as though she were nothing more than a piece of cattle he was roping.

"That'll hold her!" Delbert yelled out to Elmer, who was flying toward the steps and grabbing for the rope.

Daisy stomped and kicked and beat at the ground with her sore feet in a wild dance of protest, but she could not get free of the rope that held her prisoner.

"Simmer down!" Delbert yelled, frowning angrily at Daisy. To Elmer he said, "You won't have no more trouble now."

Elmer looked uncertain and puzzled. "What . . . what you want me to do now?" he asked Delbert.

"Take her home, boy! What you think you're supposed to do, stand around here all day?" Delbert exploded as he shoved the rope toward Elmer.

Elmer looked down at the rope. "Er . . . you mean, with the rope?"

"You don't want her to get away again, do you?" Delbert asked.

"Well, heck . . . heck no," Elmer answered, taking the rope from Delbert. He started walking slowly out of the yard and down the road, pulling Daisy along behind him with the rope. Every now and then he glanced back at Daisy and sent a mean curse falling through the air. Sometimes he yanked hard on the rope so that Daisy stumbled forward, almost falling. Those times he tossed his head back and laughed. He felt powerful now.

Along the road, on the porches of the scattered shacks and houses, people stood up to peer at Elmer and to stare with curious interest at what he was pulling behind him with the rope. Mert Potts, who had been shelling peas into a bucket beside her chair, stood up, shook out her apron, and went to the edge of the porch to gaze out at the road.

"Ain't that Elmer Goots coming there?" Mert asked her husband, Ike, who was asleep, his chair balanced precariously against the wall of the house.

Ike did not answer and when the figure on the road got closer, Mert saw that it was indeed Elmer Goots and he was pulling something by a long rope. Mert raised her hand over her forehead to shield her eyes from the sun and gazed even harder. When she saw that what Elmer was pulling was that strange creature of a child that belonged to Jessee Heath, she turned to Ike. "Would you look yonder?" When Ike only snored in response, Mert kicked the leg of his chair, and he dropped forward and woke just as the chair made a loud thump on the rough wood floor.

"What'd you do that for?" Ike demanded.

"Look out at the road," Mert told him.

Ike craned his neck and squinted his eyes, taking in Elmer. "What's that boy pulling?" he asked Mert.

"It's that slow-brained girl of Jessee Heath's," Mert answered.

"You mean that young'un that don't talk?" Ike asked, leaning forward.

"That's who I mean."

When Elmer began passing in front of the house, Ike stood up and called out, "What you doing there, boy?"

Elmer turned to grin at the old couple on the porch and answered, "I got me this here little no-account from old man Heath. I'm taking her home so's she can cook and do for me and Ma."

"That young'un is a human being! You treat her

like one!" Ike came back with a deep frown on his whiskery face.

Elmer kept walking, pulling and yanking on the rope until he had passed the house. Mert and Ike sat back down and Mert went to shelling peas again and dropping them into the bucket.

"That young'un ain't fit to of married and Elmer Goots is the worst boy in the world for her to of married!" Mert mumbled over her peas.

Ike tilted his chair back against the wall. "It's that white-haired Jessee's fault. Wanted to get rid of that girl, that's what," he said.

"And Delbert's too. Don't forget Delbert," Mert said and she dropped a handful of peas into the bucket with a sigh.

The dry, hard road hurt Daisy's feet. They were so cut and swollen and blistered. Where the rope was tied around her waist, it seemed to be cinching her breath right out of her. Her heart ached as much as her feet did. How could this be happening to her, she wondered with a deep, horrible sadness. If only she could break free! Run! But even if she did, where could she run to now? They would only start looking for her again and find her and bring her back to him. Her husband! Elmer Goots. She was so tired and weary that she was almost grateful when they reached Elmer's house and she could set down.

Elmer left Daisy tied to the front porch post while he went inside the house to let Olive know he was there. A big pepper tree with branches that sprawled over the house shaded the porch from the sun. Daisy slumped on the steps and leaned her head low over her knees, glad to feel the coolness of the shade on her. She closed her eyes and pushed her hair out of her face and in a little while began to breathe normally.

Uncontrollable thoughts knocked at Daisy's brain again. Thoughts of running away and away and away into a soft world where she would be protected, where there would never be an Elmer Goots. If she tried now, she thought, maybe she could reach up and untie the rope from the post. Maybe there would be time. She gazed up at the big knot in the rope Elmer had made around the post. It didn't look tight at all. If she tugged on it a little and slipped the end through the loop, she would be free. Slowly, holding her breath, she raised her hand toward it.

The screen door clanked behind her and she jerked her hand down into her lap and covered it with her other one. Olive Goots crossed the porch and stood towering above Daisy, her small, dark eyes roving over her with contempt and hatred. Daisy lowered her head and her hair fell over her face like a blanket, separating her from the old woman's hateful stare. But her hair blanket could not separate her from her horrible guilt, the unspeakable sin that Olive Goots made her feel she had committed.

After a moment that Daisy thought would never pass, she saw Olive's clumpy old shoes going down the steps beside her and her long print apron swishing past. She raised her head and watched through the strands of long hair as Olive walked across the yard and out to the road with quick, impatient steps. In her hand she carried an old knitting bag that bulged with clothes. The screen door opened again and every muscle in Daisy's body tightened.

"Ma's gone to spend a few days with aunt Delphine. Me and you is all alone now, Daisy-Mean-As-A-Hornet," Elmer said and all the blood inside Daisy seemed to curdle. Elmer reached for the rope to untie it from the post. Then, holding tightly to it and feeling all the power Delbert had bestowed upon him when he handed him the rope, he yanked Daisy up from the steps and shoved her through the door of the house and into a chair in the center of the front room.

Daisy stared up fearfully from beneath her eyelashes, watching Elmer as he walked around her, surveying her, up and down, and from side to side, with his evil-looking eyes.

"You ain't worth no ten dollars," Elmer said finally, stopping in front of her. "Hell! You ain't worth even *two* durned old dollars! Did you ever take a look at yourself in a mirror? I ain't seen no uglier gal in my whole put-together life! You sure is one for the books! No wonder your ol' stepdaddy wanted to get rid of you!" He chuckled. "He couldn't stand to have you around to have to look at all the time. And besides all that, he wanted to get your purty ma alone again."

Daisy looked down at the long rope lying on the floor like a snake, dangling from her waist. Suddenly she thought of the small green snake she had seen at Granny Henry's one hot summer morning. It was in a tree, dangling from a branch, and it had frightened her so that she had run to Granny Henry and Granny Henry had pulled her by her arm all the way to the window where she had been standing and pointed to the snake. "That's a garden snake, Daisy Flowerdew. It won't harm you. Fact of the matter is, it'll take off away from you if you get too close to it," Granny Henry had told her with her arm around her. Then, Granny Henry had turned her so that she was looking directly into her eyes and she added, "But they is some snakes that will strike at you as soon as you come near, child. They can kill with one bite. They is some human snakes too. They're as deadly as the ones that crawl on the ground and you have to be just as careful of them."

Daisy looked up into Elmer's eyes. She knew he was a human snake.

"I don't know how I can stand it," Elmer said staring back at her, "but I'm going to bed you down, then I'm going to put you to work around here for me and Ma. You're going to be our servant and you're going to wait on us just like we was the King and Queen of England!" He stopped and laughed and slapped at his thigh and went on. "You're going to do all the things around here Ma has been complaining about not getting done. I'm going to pay you back for that old Delbert making me marry you!"

Daisy jumped up out of the chair, crying from way down deep in her throat, but Elmer pushed her back down. "You ain't going nowhere!" he yelled in her face. He reached down and yanked the rope from around her waist, pulled her up by her shoulders, and jerked her toward the bedroom door.

Daisy stared through the door in horror. Her eyes took in an old bed with a rumpled cover, a chair with the stuffing falling out of the arms, and a clutter of clothes on the floor. She drew back, pushing and shoving against Elmer. His hands pinched into her flesh as she kicked at his legs. "Terence! Oh, Terence!" The name screamed out from inside Daisy. Elmer grabbed her arm. All at once the front door sprang open and hit the wall with a loudness that was deafening. Elmer jerked his head around at the same time Daisy did. There, standing in the doorway, lit up like lightning against the dimness of the room, Terence stood.

"What the. . . ," Elmer exploded, but the rest of his words hung caught in his throat.

"Terence!" Daisy cried with relief soaring through her.

"Let her go!" Terence demanded as he held out his hand to Daisy. She started to run to him, but Elmer held onto her arm.

"Where do you think you're going?" he snarled savagely.

Instantly, Terence came between them and, with one swoop of his hand, knocked Elmer's hand from Daisy's arm. Elmer cried out in pain, holding his arm, as Terence pulled Daisy into the depths of his broad maroon cape and, together, they ran from the house.

It seemed to Daisy that her feet did not even touch

the ground as they ran or, if they did, she felt no pain. It seemed also, somehow, that they were flying away and away and away and that Terence's cape was their wings that kept them aloft in the sky. She could feel the wind in her face and stirring through her hair as though it were soft, cool, clear water washing all her pain away.

"Where are we going, Terence?" she asked against the wind and Terence answered, "Where you've wanted to go, Daisy. *Away*."

Joy soared all through Daisy. "Oh, I'm so glad you come to get me, Terence!" Daisy cried out to the white clouds that floated by. "SOOOOO GLAAAD!"

"I promised you I would come, Daisy," Terence said as they rose higher and higher into the mist of the clouds.

"Away and away and away," Daisy said with a smile as her soul trembled with happiness. Away and away, to the away place where Granny Henry said she should run to. And maybe Granny Henry would be there waiting for her! Away, away.

Chapter
Twenty-four

Cooney Rawls and Beadie Brown, in town shopping, stopped and looked up at the sky at the same time. Something was flying overhead with great maroon-colored wings and it had a head of maroon too, and all at once, even as they watched, it seemed to rise higher and higher until it disappeared into the big white puffy clouds.

Cooney looked at Beadie, frowning and scratching at the frizzy curls on her head. "Did you ever see a bird like that before?" she asked.

"Not in all my life," Beadie answered, feeling odd. "But you know, life is full of all kinds of strangeness."

"Nothing that strange," Cooney said, frowning even more and shaking her head. "It gives me the shivers just to watch it."

The two women looked at each other for a long moment, then Beadie said in a low, cautious voice, "Did that bird look like to you that it had *four* feet?"

"Why, yes, it did. And . . . well, don't laugh, but it looked to me like they was two with boots on and two without no shoes."

Beadie threw her head back and laughed. "Who ever heard of a *bird* with boots on?"

Cooney laughed along with Beadie, but inside, they each felt a strange uneasiness, as though they had seen something that could not possibly be true and yet, they had *both* seen it. Hadn't they?

Chapter
Twenty-five

Not an hour later, Elmer Goots ran up the street like a rampaging bull and stormed into Heath's Dry Goods Store. Delbert and several customers in the store looked up and frowned in puzzlement. Elmer had never looked so distraught and disheveled. His shirt was dripping out of his pants on one side, his hair sprang in all directions, and the look on his face was as wild as his red hair.

"Where's Daisy?" he demanded in a panting, breathless yell. "You got Daisy here?"

Delbert came from around the counter, looking hard at Elmer. "What do you mean, do I have Daisy here? Last time I seen that gal, you was pulling her off my place with a rope around her waist."

"She's gone! Flat out gone!" Elmer yelled again. "Some feller busted right into my house and took her off!"

The customers in the store gathered up into a little knot and stared at Elmer.

"What are you jabbering about?" Delbert asked and his voice was high and nervous-sounding.

"I'm telling you, some feller wearing a big old maroon-colored cape and funny-looking boots come and took Daisy right out of my house!" Elmer's words shook as much as he did.

"Sounds like a tall tale to me, Elmer Goots! You sure you ain't been sneaking drinks out behind Silas Judd's Pool Hall?" Agatha Jorden asked with a skeptical, sideways look at Elmer.

"He's tooted up, all right," Bobby Gene Williams whispered to no one in particular.

"I'm telling you—" Elmer started again, but Delbert cut in with "Simmer down now! What kind of story you trying to tell here?"

Elmer sighed deeply and hit his thigh hard with his doubled fist. "How many danged, dad-burned times do I have to repeat myself?"

"Now, take it easy," Delbert said. He had to admit, Elmer was upset. There might be something to this after all, he thought. He rubbed his chin hard while studying Elmer. Beside him, Agatha Jorden and Bobby Gene Williams rubbed their chins.

"Daisy seemed to know that feller too," Elmer went on. "She run right to him the minute she seen him."

Delbert closed the store at once and drove home with a streak of dust flying behind the old car. He couldn't be sure if what Elmer was telling him was the truth but, if Daisy was gone, Jessee needed to know about it, he decided. He pulled into the front of the house and Jessee got up from the porch steps where she had been pin curling her hair, with a big smile on her face.

"What are you doing home so early, honey bear? You ain't supposed to catch me putting up my hair," Jessee said with her face flushed in pretty, pink embarrassment.

Delbert got out of the car and slammed the door. "Daisy's gone," he said as he walked toward the house.

Jessee's smile faded. She dropped her hand from her hair, a bobby pin fell out, and a wet hank of white hair dripped down over her forehead. "She's runned away again?" she cried.

"That's what Elmer said. He come into the store just a while ago and told it. He said some feller took Daisy."

Jessee grimaced in disbelief. "I know where Daisy is," she said as she grabbed the hanging strand of hair, quickly twisted it around her finger, and held it in place while she shoved her hand into her dress pocket, pulled out a bobby pin, and jabbed it into the curl. "She's down at Toby's Creek," she ended, whipping a red-and-black plaid bandana from around her shoulders and tying it over her head.

But when Jessee and Delbert went to look, they found no trace of Daisy at Toby's Creek. They called and called and trekked along the bank looking under and behind every bush and tree, but she was nowhere to be found. "We might as well go on back to the house," Delbert said at last, when evening darkness was settling over everything.

Jessee left the creek grudgingly, feeling empty and strange. As they walked back to the house she said to Delbert, "Daisy's got to be somewhere around here."

"Not if someone took her off," Delbert said.

"Who would take Daisy anywhere?" Jessee asked, looking up at Delbert with her eyes wide and frightened. They walked a little way up behind the house and Jessee said, "Maybe I was too hard on Daisy."

"No," Delbert said and he put his arm around her. "You did what you could."

"But maybe if . . . if I . . ." Jessee's words stabbed painfully at her throat. "If I could of just been *nicer* . . ."

"Don't think about it," Delbert said.

Jessee looked out across the yard where the field of low grass and scattered sprigs of wildflowers grew and could see only the barren nothingness of her motherhood. She began to weep softly.

"Ain't no need to cry," Delbert told her, patting her shoulder.

"I weren't no good mother," Jessee said, wiping at her eyes with her fingertips.

"Don't say that."

"I weren't no good mother!" Jessee screamed, looking up at Delbert's stunned face. She turned and started to run back to the woods, but Delbert grabbed her arm and pulled her to him.

"You can blame yourself for Daisy or you can accept facts," he said sternly. "And the facts is, there weren't nothing you could do that could of helped that young'un. She weren't right in her head and she didn't look right. She was a freak of nature."

Jessee stopped weeping and said in a low, painful whisper, "I could of tried . . . tried to love her. Just of tried."

Neither one of them spoke again the rest of the way to the house.

All through the night Jessee slept and woke, slept and woke, and wondered where Daisy could be. Maybe Elmer had done something to her, she thought at times. Or maybe what he said was true. Maybe someone did take Daisy, just like he claimed had happened. But more than likely, she concluded, before going back to sleep for the last time, Daisy had simply run away. It was easier for Jessee to sleep thinking that. It meant Daisy had made a choice in what happened to her, that she hadn't been taken against her will. Thinking that, she fell asleep and stayed asleep until morning.

Chapter
Twenty-six

The next day Cooney Rawls and Beadie Johnson went into the dry goods store and told Delbert what they had seen in the sky the day before. Or what they *thought* they had seen. They still questioned it and had debated over three cups of coffee and four fat blueberry muffins apiece if they should keep such a story to themselves or tell Delbert. Word had spread around town that Daisy was missing and they wondered if there could be some connection. After all, hadn't they heard tell that Elmer had said the person who took Daisy was wearing a maroon-colored cape? And hadn't that *bird,* or *whatever* it was, *looked* maroon-colored?

"We'll be the laughingstock of Vineyard Flats if we tell such a story!" Beadie had said at first.

"It's our Christian duty to tell what we know," Cooney said back.

Finally, after much consultation, muffins, and coffee, the two ladies entered the store, found Delbert alone, and related what they had seen to him.

Delbert's mouth fell open. "Did you say a *maroon bird*?"

"With four feet," Cooney and Beadie said in unison and they both laughed a little, feeling embarrassed to admit such foolishness.

Delbert's eyes grew huge as he stared at the two women. *"Four feet?"* he managed to ask when he could get his mouth back into working order.

"And two of them had old-timey-looking boots on them with shiny-looking buckles," Cooney said.

"And the other two didn't have no shoes on and the feet was small, like a girl's feet," Beadie added.

"And . . . and it seemed to disappear right into the clouds," Cooney continued.

Delbert rushed to the door of the store and peered up into the sky. He had no idea what he was looking for, but his eyes searched the clouds and blueness of the sky and stared at them for a long, long time. Behind him, Cooney and Beadie exchanged several looks, coughed, and cleared their throats, waiting for Delbert to return from the door. After a while, Cooney went to the counter where a box of embroidery thread was displayed and selected several skeins. After a while longer, she began to thump the skeins of embroidery thread back and forth between her fingers and to frown at Delbert's back. Beside her, Beadie whispered, "The man appears to be in shock."

Finally Delbert returned from the door and went behind the counter.

"Well," Cooney said, shoving the embroidery thread across the counter to him, "I reckon we didn't really see a thing but the sun in the clouds playing tricks on our eyes."

"Why, yes," Beadie said, "that had to be it."

Delbert said nothing. He rang up the sale on the cash register automatically, placed the thread in a bag, and shoved it across to Cooney.

Once more, Delbert closed the store early and went bounding home in a swirl of dust, this time almost colliding with a hay wagon just making a turn off Dogtown Road. He pulled into the yard and jumped out of the car almost before it stopped and went flying up the steps of the porch and into the house. He told Jessee what Cooney and Beadie had related to him as soon as his feet touched the floor inside the house.

"Oh, my Lord in heaven!" Jessee gasped, jumping up and running through the house to the back room where Daisy had slept. Delbert was right at her heels, yelling out, "Where are you going? What's wrong?"

Jessee did not answer and when she reached the back-porch room, she leaned down and pulled a small book from under Daisy's mattress. When she raised up, Delbert was beside her breathing hard, with an impatient frown on his face.

"Just today I found this little book of poems under Daisy's mattress. It was Ma's. I don't know why Daisy had it." She held the book up for Delbert to see.

"Well?" Delbert demanded impatiently.

Jessee opened the book and turned the pages quickly, her eyes skittering across each page.

"What are you doing?" Delbert demanded again and he tried to snatch the book from Jessee's hands, but she turned away, shielding the book, and said, "Just a minute, honey bear! I want to read you something that I read when I found the book."

Delbert sighed loudly and gave Jessee a sharp, annoyed look. A fine time to be reading poetry, he thought disgustedly.

"Oh, here it is. Now, honeybee, listen to this carefully. You listen real hard while I read. It's a poem," Jessee said when she had found the page she was looking for.

"I don't want to hear no poem!" Delbert roared.

"Just listen!" Jessee cried.

Delbert sighed again and slumped down on Daisy's cot. He watched Jessee's pretty, expressive face as she opened her mouth and began to read.

"The name of this poem, honey bear, is 'The Paper Doll Boy,' and here's the way it goes:

> *The flower wilted, so near death it was*
> *But with one last breath, its feeble petal*
> *Raised and called*
> *And the Paper Doll Boy, becoming real because*
> *The flower's heart did break, rose like the*
> *Sun and rode the wind to the daisy's rescue*
> *His billowing cape, a cloud of maroon, flowing*
> *Behind him. . . .*

Delbert jumped up and grabbed the book from

Jessee's hands. His lips began to tremble and struggle over the unfamiliar words. "'As . . . as o–one t–they sped the waves and d–dis–disappeared into t–the wel–welcoming clouds.'" He looked up at Jessee, snapping the book closed and feeling that he had met a strangeness in life that made him weak and unclear in his mind.

"It . . . it don't mean a thing!" he said in a low voice, but he was as white as Jessee's bleached hair.

Slowly Jessee bent down and raised the corner of Daisy's pillow and pulled out the envelope that said "For the Parlor Amusement of Little Girls" and opened it to peer inside. The envelope was empty. She looked up at Delbert, who could only stare back at her. She reached for the other envelope, opened it, and found Grace lying flat with her smiling face and eyes looking directly into Jessee's. Jessee frowned.

"What's wrong?" Delbert asked in that same low voice.

"Nothing," Jessee answered. But somehow, it seemed to Jessee that the paper doll's face had changed, that the smile and the eyes were different, almost as if they were mocking Jessee for some secret reason. She pulled Grace all the way out of the envelope and held her in her hand. "The boy doll's gone," she went on, still looking at Grace's smiling face.

"So what?" Delbert said nervously.

"Well, I don't know what," Jessee answered.

"I do." Grace said, without changing her expression. But no one heard her.

 *Epilogue*

No one in Vineyard Flats really knew what happened to Daisy Flowerdew. There were some who said she got away from Elmer Goots and ran back to Toby's Creek and, in her desperation, fell in, drowning. Others surmised that she ran from the town and was picked up by a band of Gypsies, taken against her will, and forced to live with them. Others whispered that Elmer had killed Daisy and buried her in some distant, silent place where no one would ever go. Still, there were others who hoped in their secret hearts that Daisy had found a pleasant, secure place to go where she could live out her life in peaceful happiness.

Time moved on and the years fled away and Daisy was rarely mentioned. People came to accept that, perhaps she did, after all, fall into Toby's Creek and drown. Even Delbert and Jessee, who kept the book of poems safely tucked away in a dresser drawer and spoke of it to no one, soon released the poem into a little secret cranny of their minds and left it there, covered and still and voiceless. After all, who would ever accept such a far-fetched story as true? Even Cooney Rawls and Beadie Brown changed their story to each other and decided upon an easier one to live with: that the sun had, indeed, been in their eyes that day when they were looking into the sky and *thought* they had seen a maroon bird with four feet.

Sometimes Yule Shipton, the paper doll agent, is seen on the roads of Vineyard Flats, but he never stops at Jessee and Delbert's place. It is as if, somehow, he knows Daisy is no longer there. As for Grace, she lives to this day in her envelope home, pressed beneath a clutter of old magazines on a shelf in Jessee's closet, a smile still on her face.